Tomb of the Kobold King
Darkshield Volume II
By Kathe Todd

Tomb of the Kobold King by Kathe Todd. The Darkshield Series, Volume 2. Copyright © 2015, 2016 by Kathe Todd. No portion may be reproduced by any means without the permission of the copyright holder. Published by Kalefaction Press, an imprint of Rip Off Press. Visit KatheTodd.com for contact information and the full list of titles available. First print edition March 2016. ISBN: 978-0-89620-031-9

Chapter 1

Adara gazed ahead of her to the south and east as Zarhya, Sadiq in tow behind her, clattered over the Willough Bridge heading for Rivermarch. It was a beautiful summer morning, but she gazed upon her home duchy with a trace of sadness. Last night for her stay in Grandwyl she had opted *not* to room at the Duke's Head inn. Not only could she now afford accommodations many times richer, but memories of her first time there, making love with Ferdyn, would have been bittersweet. For Ferdyn did not accompany her on this trip home.

We were the victims of our own success, Adara sighed to herself as she turned east from the bridge and began retracing the route she and her companion had traveled only three months before. Though they had not taken *all* of the Swinzen gold from within the treasure room in the Bloodspire, they had brought back enough of it to let both of them live like royalty for the rest of their lives.

Adara had never known want, and Ferdyn's family were comfortably well off. But now they were both rich beyond dreams of avarice. When they'd returned to the royal palace in Carlienne to report their triumph to Cruztan Milegos, he had brought the news to His Majesty King Arden of Tanar. And suddenly, the young couple were the darlings of the capital.

Ferdyn bought a handsome town house in the Palace District for them to live in, just the two of them and a staff of servants. They were presented with medals at court, thanking them for their service to the realm – for had the late Mancer King Sarand Bloodspire fulfilled his ambitions, the kingdom would have become just a province of the evil magus' empire.

And everyone, especially the younger members of Tanar's nobility, were eager to befriend them. They were wined and dined and invited to lavish parties, offered partnerships in prestigious firms, and courted by sycophants wishing to claim that Ferdyn and Adara were their close personal friends. "And I'll be invited to the wedding, I hope?"

Yes, everyone including Ferdyn assumed that he and Adara would soon be wed – ready to take up an urban lifestyle suited to their wealth and position. For a while Adara had been swept up in the heady whirl of it all – meeting new people who all seemed to love her, dressing in gorgeous gowns, riding around in elegant carriages, being waited on hand and foot.

But after a month or so, though thanks to her enchanted ring she had easily learned how to create the appearance of being a part of that social set, Adara knew in her heart that it was all a charade. And it was not what she wanted from life. "Ferdyn, I'm not yet eighteen!" she had told him. "I'm not through having adventures yet. With all this money at my command I can explore the world for learning's sake, maybe even make significant contributions to knowledge."

Ferdyn hadn't been able to understand. What was the point of adventuring, if not to take home treasure? True, exploring ancient tombs had a thrill that went beyond what loot you might discover – and ridding the world of bandit gangs was a service to society. But at the point where he'd opened his bank account, depositing his share of the gold bars and assuring that he would never have to work a day in his life again, he'd realized that without money as a motivation he no longer really wanted to go out and sleep in the cold and damp, risking his life, just to see what was out there.

It had nearly broken Adara's heart. She loved him still, and their relationship was still passionate – when they found time to make love, in among the social whirl. But Ferdyn had changed, had become somebody different from the man she had fallen in love with. And so, she had left him.

Not finally, it was true. They had parted sadly, with one last rip-roaring fuck for remembrance, before she had set off astride her mare – with the newly acquired gelding for a pack horse – on the journey back to Pine Hill to reunite with Nanny Selden. So far as anyone in that remote Rivermarch village knew, the young woman they'd outfitted for a trip to the capital months ago had vanished without a trace. News was slow to arrive in the hinterlands.

But deep in her heart, Adara knew, there would be no going back to that aimless, meaningless life of indulgence and luxury in Carlienne. And unless Ferdyn changed his mind, that meant no returning to his arms. But oh, how she missed him! Each night of her journey along the river road, as she laid herself down to sleep in the best inn beds available, Adara had tears on her cheeks and an aching in her heart. That wasn't the only place that ached. Now that the recent ex-virgin had become accustomed to an active sex life, the lack of a vigorous man in her bed was becoming more and more of an issue. It was a good thing that Ferdyn had taught her ways in which she could pleasure herself!

Adara heaved another, deeper, sigh and put her heels to Zarhya, getting her and her in-tow companion to pick up the pace a little as they moved along the hard-packed dirt road that lay along the southern bank of the Willough. The trip so far had been civilized, inns well-spaced along the Grandeon's north bank between Carlienne and Grandwyl. But the north side of Rivermarch offered little. There were no inns, and no habitations of man, between here and Pine Hill nearly a hundred miles away.

Excitement rose in Adara as she sharpened her awareness, looking all around her. For the first time in weeks she felt truly alive – at peril, facing the world with nothing but her own resources to defend her. Admittedly those resources included the Darkshield, an ancient magical artifact that shielded her from all hostile magic; and what she had come to call the Learning Ring – which enabled her to learn almost anything, be it skill or lore, in a fraction of the time one might expect. After a few weeks of practice she was an expert swordswoman, an expert rider. And anything else she might set her hand to would come as easily. Adara sent a little prayer of thanks to Mother Maridem as she rode along, that the Royal Magus Cruztan Milagros had seen fit to give her such a gift.

Chapter 2

That night found Adara and her equine entourage far to the east of where she and Ferdyn had camped, that last night before reaching Grandwyl a few months ago. She sighed as she set about putting the horses to rights, laying a campfire, and pitching the excellent small tent she had bought from a Carlienne firm that claimed to be Tanar's finest outfitters – recalling how Ferdyn had done all these chores while they were traveling together.

Get over it, girl, she told herself, though truth to tell she felt a powerful loneliness as she set about making a camp stew for one. The horses offered companionship of a sort, but she couldn't really carry on a conversation with them. Nor would they warm her bed.

Adara had not shared any of those inn beds along the river road from Carlienne to Grandwyl with anyone, though she had certainly had offers. The human interaction in the common rooms of those inns had been enough to satisfy her desire for companionship, and she had not been ready to take another lover. Especially since it was likely any liaison along the road would have been nothing but a one-night stand.

Now, though, she was beginning to think that it would be nice to hook up with a traveling companion before embarking on the first adventure she planned once she'd visited Pine Hill and checked in at Willoughby. Somebody to enjoy camaraderie with around the campfire in the evenings, somebody to watch her back; somebody to fill the aching in her loins. Mmm, maybe Jason Miller might be interested in coming along with her. He was not really needed around the mill…

The night was warm, and Adara extinguished her campfire before lying down in her bedroll for the night. She kept her bow, quiver, and Voleur near to hand, counting on the horses to alert her to any intruders. After lying down she closed her eyes, but did not immediately sleep. Instead, she reached out her awareness, curious about what might be stirring in the area. If a pack of wolves were roaming nearby, it might be wise to learn of it before falling asleep!

Though Adara's riding ability did not allow her to go inside the minds of sentient creatures like men and elves, she had developed it far beyond what Nanny had ever taught her. She had discovered with the Fatiha Baba, that magical necklace that could open permanent portals to other dimensions, that under certain circumstances she could communicate mind to mind if a sentience was willing to accept the connection. It now rested at the bottom of her pack and she had not tried to use it again, fearful of the power and its implications.

So far, that enchanted artifact – evidently infused with a human soul in its creation – was the only sentience with which she'd been able to thus communicate. Trying to enter the minds of most humans, she met only an impenetrable barrier like an invisible shield – the person's self-awareness, preventing her from making contact. But maybe someday she might meet another person with his ability she had, and if they were reaching out for her as she was reaching out for them, they might be able to communicate by telepathy. How amazing would *that* be?

Lying as if in a trance, flat on her back, Adara extended her awareness out within a circle ten miles in diameter. She could look much further, but this was the practical limit for a general scan. The number of living creatures, large and small, in an area of nearly eighty square miles, was almost too much for her to encompass. As it was she ignored the insects, the little roosting songbirds, the mice and wood rats and the owls that hunted them. She was on the lookout for creatures large enough to menace her, especially if they should be on the prowl while she was sleeping.

Almost due east, and near the limit of her scan, Adara spotted a party of three humans – grown men from the glow they made in her mental vision. She pushed, trying to see if she could detect any emanations of intent. Sometimes people could radiate their feelings, if they were strong enough.

Getting nothing, she searched the immediate area. There, some hundred feet away from what she assumed was their campsite, a stoat was stalking a meadow mouse. Adara entered it and took control, the creature's burning hunger momentarily shoved to the back of its mind as she filled it with the desire to approach the humans nearby.

Slithering through the undergrowth, silent on its little paws, the weasel saw a campfire ahead. Adara brought it forward until the entire campsite became visible. It had been set up on the bank between the river and the road, with little in the way of cover around it.

Three men sat around the fire on driftwood logs, drinking something out of tankards and talking softly. Adara felt another stab of loneliness. Clearly, she was not cut out to be a social butterfly. But she wasn't meant to be a hermit, either. They were dressed in respectable-looking traveling clothes and appeared to be armed only with daggers. Their conversation was in Franca, and revolved around the money they hoped to get for the leather goods on their pack mules.

Good, not bandits then. Adara let the stoat go back about his business, before his high metabolism should leave him literally fainting with hunger. She looked here and there, but found no more humans within her circle. On the far side of the Willough though, on a weathered rock promontory, Adara spotted a mind that was almost but not quite sentient. There was a small group of them, one larger and three smaller. A wolf pack, perhaps?

Projecting an aura of peace, of relaxation, Adara slipped past the creature's resistance and looked out through its eyes. Oh, how cute! The alert creature was a mother, and she had three well-grown babies nursing at her side. They appeared to be in a rock den, a hemispherical gouge probably high up on a cliff face overlooking the river's north bank. For this was no wolf.

The mother and her babies were semigryphs, shy creatures Adara had only seen a couple of times in her life before. They hunted mostly at night, their cats' eyes and large, pointed ears as able as any owl's to pick out small prey. But they had a taste for river fish as well, and could sometimes be seen in the crepuscular hours of dawn or dusk stooping low over the water to snatch salmon or trout in their needle-sharp, retractable front talons.

Mama semigryph's night vision enabled Adara to make out the sweet, handsomely striped faces of the kits as they nursed. The flight feathers on their as-yet stubby wings were well grown in, and it would probably not be long before they fledged. But their mother would stay with them for months yet, helping them to perfect their hunting skills before kicking them out to fend for themselves.

Full-sized gryphons were a terror, another reason besides dragons that it was better for humans to avoid traveling in the high mountains. They were little smaller than lions, with wingspans as big as any roc's. But semigryphs were no bigger than an eagle, their feline bodies like those of a particular stocky, tabby-striped house cat.

Sheep farmers claimed they sometimes took lambs, but Adara doubted that they were anywhere near the menace to livestock those farmers made out. Any farmer would likely shoot a semigryph on sight, probably one reason they were so shy. They were probably actually beneficial, killing rodents that might otherwise feed on farmers' crops. But you certainly wouldn't see any farmer keeping a family of semigryphs in his barn! Housecats were a lot more manageable.

The babies had dropped off to sleep, and the mother semigryph detached herself carefully from her brood and picked her way around them to the edge of her lair. Then she launched herself off into space, reflections of moonlight glinting off the river below as she flew across it and quested in among the trees on the hillside south of Adara's campsite.

Adara rode with her, just passively enjoying the ride, for another few minutes. The mother was an excellent hunter, catching a polecat before long. Though the creature had released its musk, it didn't seem to bother the predator much. She just swiped a paw across her nose and then dug into her meal. Ugh, her uninvited passenger thought, and pulled her awareness back home. Time she was getting to sleep.

Chapter 3

Nothing disturbed Adara and her horses during the night, and she was out of her bedroll as soon as the eastern sky had begun to get light. Nights at this season were short, but she'd had enough rest inside her comfortable tent; and she was eager to be on her way.

The trip between Pine Hill and Grandwyl that had taken five days for her to travel on old Bulo's broad back, encumbered as he was by two riders and all their belongings, would likely take Adara only three or four with her two fine Khoureshis. Sadiq was not quite the mount Zarhya was, a gelding ten years old; but he still had plenty of life left in him and she could ride him in a pinch.

After breakfasting on trail bread and water, Adara was soon packed up and ready to ride. She had decided to avoid cooking as much as possible on this trip, finding cooking for only herself to be hardly worth the bother. How had Nanny Selden managed it for all those years? The old woman had confided to her adopted daughter that she had been widowed, alone in her cottage in the woods, for nearly thirty years before Adara had come along to change her life.

Along this stretch of the river road the view to the waters of the Willough, still fairly broad this close to its mouth, was mostly clear. Just a few paces to her right the woods of the peninsula climbed sharply to the ridge dividing the Grandeon from the Willough. In a couple of days' travel the terrain would level out considerably, but for now it was as if there was a wall to Adara's south and a broad river to her north, with only a narrow strip of level land between.

Still keeping fully aware of her surroundings, ready to fend off attackers or take advantage of an opportunity for fresh game, Adara's head swiveled from side to side as Zarhya went along at a trot with Sadiq in tow behind. She looked up to the north, trying to find the semigryph den. From what she'd seen last night, it was high enough above the surface of the Willough that it should be visible from the road.

The north bank of the river was nowhere near as hilly as the south one, and it wasn't long before Adara spotted a rocky outcropping off to the east. Surely that must be it? She reined in Zarhya for a moment, to peer up into the sky. Was that the mother semigryph circling above her? They were certainly capable of soaring like eagles or condors, but it was not their preferred hunting technique.

Craning her neck, Adara spotted in profile the drawn-up hind legs and long, furry tail that were the hallmark of a semigryph in flight. A long, plaintive "Meowww!" could be heard, as the creature circled lower. The human watcher below felt a pang. Had the babies begun trying their wings, and one tumbled from the nest? She'd had plenty of opportunity to observe nature growing up, and she knew that baby animals in the wild had a low survival rate. That didn't prevent her from feeling sad at the thought of one of those adorable kits lying broken at the foot of the rocky escarpment ahead.

Though the only sensible course was to avert her eyes and push on, Adara found herself scanning the rocks at the bottom of the cliff. Near its top, she could the dark opening of the semigryph den and what she thought was two of the kits standing near the edge, peering down. It was still a bit too far away to be sure.

Suddenly the mother dived – not to the rocks at the foot of the escarpment on the far side of the stream, but to the sandy southern bank only a couple of dozen yards from the road. Her cries were urgent now, and Adara was powerless to ride on past. Taking Zarhya and Sadiq off the road, she swiftly dismounted. She tied the mare's reins to a willow and commanded "Stay." Over the nearly three months since acquiring the Khoureshi mare, Adara had learned that the horse's training went far beyond what she'd initially thought.

Pushing through the clump of willows between the road and the bank, Adara made her way toward the shore. There on a mud bank on the downstream side of a little backwater, the mother semigryph stood four-footed, wings spread, guarding her fallen fledgling. She hissed and growled as the young woman approached, and Adara backed off a little as she tried to see what the situation was.

The kit looked more than half-drowned. The Willough at this point was at least five hundred feet from bank to bank, fairly shallow and studded with large rocks. It was one of the reasons the river had no significant commerce with the rest of the kingdom. Had the baby semigryph sailed out from the nest above, only to come down in the middle of the stream and be caught by the current?

Mama semigryph nudged her lost baby, meowing anxiously at it. The kit was alive, Adara realized. Might all be well? It was almost two-thirds the size of its mother, but she seized it by the scruff of its neck and began dragging it up the bank – away from the deadly swirling waters. The kit roused from its stupor and protested vigorously, yowling in pain at being moved.

Adara realized that from the way the right wing was flopping the outer long bone – what would have been the radius in a human arm – was broken. And broken badly. Unless medical care was applied, this baby would never fly. And while a semigryph still had four feet on which to navigate, Adara knew the chances for such a creature surviving in the wild were slim.

Her emotions carried her away, and she didn't stop to work out all the possible consequences of her actions. Adara burst out of the clump of willows waving her arms and shouting, and the mother semigryph panicked and took to the air yowling out her rage. The species was well-equipped by nature with fang and claw, but they weighed barely thirty pounds to Adara's one hundred-twenty. And she was armed with a claw of her own – a gleaming length of tempered steel more than three feet long.

Adara stood over the injured kit, defying its mother, until the creature finally admitted defeat and flew off to the northeast to guard the rest of her brood. Such failures must come to every wild mother, Adara realized. Nature had made them fiercely protective, but it also told them when it was time to give it up and move on. Now Adara bent to the kit, and found it no less fierce. "Mrrowl!" it cried, in its kitten voice – getting onto its four legs and backing away from her hissing though the pain from its broken wing was so severe it was a wonder it could walk at all.

Adara didn't know what else to do, and while remaining standing and aware of her surroundings she sent her mind out to the semigryph kit. Could she take over its mind, command it to remain calm while she saw to its injuries? She had never before tried to ride a creature that was injured and in distress. The emotions were strong, hard to overcome. Adara was inside the kit's mind now, and she sent a flood – of feelings, of thoughts, of words. Though of course no non-sentient creature could understand human words.

"Be calm, be at peace. Thy pain will soon be over," Adara sent – in words and images and emotions. And the kit's mind calmed. Unexpectedly she received a message back – in images and emotions that somehow translated themselves to words in her mind: "Help me, it *hurts!*"

Adara scooped the kit up from where it lay on the sandy riverbank, and carried it in her arms back toward where the horses were tied. It weighed no more than twenty pounds, a slight and bedraggled bundle. She laid it carefully down in soft sand beside the willows where the horses were tied, and quickly pulled her pack down off of Sadiq's back.

The party of merchants, with their six pack mules in tow, came past on the road a few minutes later. They glanced at the young woman with the two fine-looking horses, bent over something they could not quite make out on the ground beneath a stand of willows, but did not call to her as they continued on their way west.

Getting the kit to lick up a little morfeo had been Adara's first step. Then she had carefully set the broken wing bone and immobilized it. Without the ability to fly, the young semigryph would never be able to live the life nature had intended for it. She then wrapped the sleepy kit in a woolen shawl, and secured it to her body in a sling. She hoped that the warmth of that body would help to calm it. Semigryphs were after all mammals, though they were one of only half a dozen species she knew of with six, not four, limbs.

Finally Adara and her horses were off again, continuing east along the river road. Mother Maridem, what was I thinking? Adara wondered. She had just taken on a wild animal, currently an invalid but soon – if it didn't simply die – a creature famed for its ferocity. How was she even going to feed it?

Chapter 4

Her motherly instincts aroused, Adara was extra-alert for game and bagged two rabbits and a good-sized squirrel in the hours before time to break for lunch. By then the dose of morfeo had worn off and the kit was beginning to stir and mewl in its cloth sling.

Adara climbed down from Zarhya's back, hastily getting the mare and her companion supplied with water. They could graze from the thick roadside grasses while she fed herself and dealt with her new charge, and there would be grain for them tonight. She had slackened the pace, not wanting to jostle the semigryph kit unduly.

All the time, an inner voice was shouting at her, "What in hell were you thinking? You can't take on a helpless baby monster!" So far, Adara had been fairly successful at ignoring that voice. She had even, discovering the kit was a girl, come up with a name for her: Malika. While Ferdyn had been throwing himself whole-heartedly into the round of socializing and gaiety in Carlienne, Adara had been exploring the uses of her Learning Ring to study as much lore as she could get her hands on. And that lore was almost unlimited, if you were situated in the kingdom's capital with a fat purse. Malika was Khoureshi for "queen," which was what female semigryphs were called.

Adara quickly gutted one of the rabbits, stripping off the skin, and began cutting little slices of meat away from the bones. From Malika's full set of needle-sharp baby teeth, she had been eating solid food for some time now. Adara sent her mind into the young semigryph's, not in full control but as more of a comforting, motherly presence. "Eat, my little one, and grow strong." The words could mean nothing to the young animal, but the emotions conveyed the meaning. With a look up into her eyes, Malika began wolfing down the gobbets of warm, red flesh as Adara provided them.

When the little semigryph was sated, and beginning to drift off again into sleep, Adara flung away the remnants of the rabbit carcass. Tucking the little one back into her sling, she dug out more trail bread to eat and took a few swigs from one of her water skins. Oh, water! Malika had not drunk. But the moisture content of the fresh meat would have provided her with some liquid. Making a mental note to force her fosterling to drink before feeding her again, Adara mounted Zarhya again and went on her way – slowly and gently.

The following morning, Malika was beginning to feel a little better. At the evening stop Adara had brewed some Boneheal tea, and after Ariel (the air elemental whose favors Adara could call on at will) had cooled it the little semigryph had been induced to lap some from the bowl she'd brought for soups, stews, and porridge.

And Adara had begun to establish a rapport with the little creature, reaching out mind to mind in a way that tread a line between the complete control of riding and the communication she'd experienced with Fatiha Baba. It seemed that semigryphs, if not entirely sentient, were far smarter than anyone had realized.

"Drink it up, it will make you better," Adara sent. And "yes, it is good," came back to her. Not words exactly, but understanding. She slept the night wrapped snug in her bedroll with Malika warm and content beside her, and both of them were the better for the contact.

Two more days Adara rode, with her baby monster growing stronger and more vociferous with every passing hour. No longer was she mooning over lost Ferdyn, or feeling her loneliness – all of her time, it seemed, was taken up addressing Malika's needs. Is this what motherhood is like? She wondered, with an unspoken prayer of thanks to Mother Maridem that so far she'd been spared that particular honor.

Malika was no longer contained within the sling, which had been reconfigured as a body-band to hold the broken wing immobile against her small, furry body. Adara had wrapped it around both wings, figuring that having both of them held tight would be less upsetting and confusing for her young charge.

With her wings confined, the young semigryph somewhat resembled the little wildcats that inhabited the forest regions of Eorla. But the expanded breastbone, attachment point for the musculature needed to power the wings, gave her a chesty appearance. And the claws on her forepaws were four times the length and strength of the claws of ordinary cats. She rode the saddle in front of Adara, looking around them with obvious interest and enjoyment – and thankfully, not sinking those impressive talons into Zarhya's tender flesh.

As their mental rapport had grown, Adara had been astounded to find that Malika was now reaching out mentally to *her*. Was that ability not after all limited to humans, to those who were considered "sentient"? Admittedly the little semigryph's sendings were mostly along the lines of "When's lunch?" and "I smell something funny." But she was *communicating* mind to mind with her adoptive mother, not simply meowing inarticulately!

It was late in the afternoon on the fourth day that Adara and her animal companions reached the juncture of the river road and the main road leading north from Pine Hill. She felt a thrill run through her at seeing the familiar intersection, and turned Zarhya's head to the south to climb the hill into town. She thought it best to take a room at the Loggers' Rest, and leave the horses there while she visited in town.

How long she would stay would depend on many things, including whether Jason Miller was up for some adventure with the girl he'd been pursuing for most of the past year. Adara got another thrill at that thought, but it was centered a little lower down.

Adara guided Zarhya around to the rear of the inn, where Mrs. Anderson's younger boy Edvard took charge of the horses and greeted her in astonishment. "Miss Selden, you've returned!" he exclaimed. Adara was only three years older than he was, but Eddy was a shy and respectful lad.

"Yep," she replied cheerfully. "I'm all in one piece, and the demon bringer is dead. Could I get you to bring my pack inside after you get the horses rubbed down?" She gave the boy a silver shilling, a handsome tip, and he goggled at her fine traveling garb, the sword riding in its back scabbard, and the semigryph at her side as she turned to go into the inn through the back door.

Finally he blurted, "Yes'm! Will do!" and turned his attention to the horses as she went inside. The boy's mother, the widow Anderson, was as astonished.

"Adara, is that you?" she asked. I've only been gone for a little over three months, Adara thought. But those three months had wrought many changes in her. She was clad in the new traveling

16

clothes she'd had made for her in Carlienne – snug-fitting, supple leather pants with a reinforced crotch, and a leather vest armored front and back with light, strong irilium plates. Certainly a bit more exotic than what she'd been wearing on her departure.

Adara smiled at the motherly woman. "Hello Mistress Anderson," she said warmly. "I'm here for a visit. How is Nanny doing?" Gertrude Anderson leaned over the bar and peered down at Malika, who was sitting on her haunches and looking about with interest. Her nose was twitching, and she sent "I smell something *good*!"

"We'll eat soon," Adara sent back. For a member of a notoriously shy and cautious wild species, the little semigryph seemed to be taking her first trip inside a dwelling of men with equanimity. Perhaps it was her mental bond with Adara, and Adara's utter lack of concern about coming inside, that let her remain so calm.

"Is that a wildcat?" the innkeeper asked with a trace of anxiety. With her wings wrapped tight around her body by the length of cloth, Malika *did* quite resemble one of the little forest wildcats that shared the semigryphs' range if not their hunting techniques.

Adara grinned. Oh, it was so much *fun* to return to sleepy little Pine Hill and blow everyone's minds! "Malika is a semigryph," she explained. "She has a broken wing and I'm nursing her back to health. I expect in a few months when she's finished growing up and can fly, she'll leave me and go back to the wild. But for now, she seems to have attached herself to me."

"Will wonders never cease?" the innkeeper mused. Then she recalled Adara had asked after Nanny Selden. Of course! "Nanny's just fine, dear," she told the tall young woman with a smile. "I swear, she'll outlive us all. She was already well up in age when I was a youngster, but she just keeps going strong. Young Ellie Forrest is apprenticing with her now, as you know, and her mother's given her permission to live with Nanny full time now. You may be wanting to room here, I'm afraid."

"I'd expected to," Adara told her matter-of-factly, though she felt a little pang. To have been replaced so quickly and easily, booted out of the only home she had known for much of her life until recently! She dispelled the feeling with a mental shrug. She'd come back to Pine Hill with absolutely no intention of taking up her old life again. She was an adult, and the career path she'd always expected to follow no longer held much allure.

At this juncture Edvard came in through the back door lugging Adara's heavy pack. "I'll take whichever is your largest room," Adara told the innkeeper. She had eaten here many times but had never even been inside any of the inn's four guest rooms. The night with Ferdyn at the Duke's Head in Grandwyl had been her first ever stay in such an establishment. She was willing to bet that the amenities offered by Mistress Anderson would be a little more rustic than those at the Duke's Head, but she at least hoped she might be able to get a hot bath tonight.

After Adara's pack had been ensconced in her room, she changed into a clean skirt and blouse and some shoes appropriate for walking in. Voleur stayed in the room, but she belted a ten-inch irilium dagger at her side. This gleaming silvery metal was harder, stronger, and lighter than steel, held an edge well, and was not subject to rust. It was also very difficult to work, and only Elven smiths and those trained by them knew how to do so. This dagger, her traveling vest, and the set of plate mail tucked away in her pack together had cost more than the average shopkeeper brought home in five years.

"I'm going over to Pine Trading to pick up a few things, then out to Nanny's," Adara told Mistress Anderson. "Likely I'll be there for dinner, but I expect to be back here to sleep for the night." As soon as they'd been let into the room Malika had hopped up onto the double bed, curled up, and gone to sleep. Semigryphs were usually considered to be nocturnal, after all; though traveling with Adara had warped the young creature's daily schedule.

Adara was tempted to just let her nap, but decided against it. Without her nearby to commune with and calm her, Malika's wild nature might cause problems. As she walked up Pine Hill's main street toward the general store, the not-quite cat scampered at her side.

A bell attached to the door tinkled as Adara stepped inside. "I'm in the back," came a voice, "Be with you in a minute!" She recognized the voice as belonging to Nelly Green, a girl not quite a year younger than she was who worked with her widowed mother running the family business.

Adara looked around her at the store's contents with new eyes. This place had once been a repository of wonders to her, stocking manufactured goods from far-off places as well as locally made homespun cloth, fruits, vegetables, and smoked meats from the area farms, and items like Nanny's potions. Now that she had spent a couple of months living in Carlienne, the jumbled collection of merchandise offered for sale seemed… quaint. But it gave her a nostalgic jolt as well, taking her back to her childhood.

Malika sniffed eagerly, poking her inquisitive nose into this and that as Adara strolled the aisles looking for items she might like to buy for Nanny. Hm, definitely one of those hams. And this brightly-dyed woolen shawl, while too warm for summer, would make a lovely gift that would be enjoyed when autumn came in a few months…

Suddenly Adara heard a male voice say, "Adara? How…" She glanced up to see the very person who had been so much in her thoughts, all alone in her bedroll during the journey from Grandwyl. Technically Malika had shared her bedroll on several of those nights, but…

"Jason! How good to see you!" Adara caroled, stepping over to give him a little hug.

Considering that kiss he'd delivered at their last parting, she'd expected him to enfold her in an enthusiastic embrace. Instead he stepped backward as she approached him, putting his hands on her shoulders as if to fend her off. What? Now he was giving her an embarrassed grin, and looking out of the corner of his eye at the door to the back room.

Oho, had he been chatting up Nelly Green in her absence? Considering that Adara had enthusiastically surrendered her maidenhead to another man and had been living with him as if married (but without benefit of ceremony) for the past couple of months, she supposed she could scarcely complain. She had no more claim on Jason than he did on her – she had not even committed to letting him escort her to the Spring Dance when last they'd parted.

But she had definitely been casting Jason in the role of her next lover, a role she expected he would be happy to fulfill considering how much effort he'd put in trying to get into her drawers over the past year. Nelly emerged from the storeroom at the back, saw the two of them standing close together and threw a furious glance at Adara, then at Jason. He backed off still further.

"Look dear, Adara's returned to us," Jason said weakly.

"How nice," Nelly replied coolly. "Are you back to stay, or will you be leaving us again soon?" she asked in a tone that suggested the latter choice would be favorite. Adara didn't miss that, nor had she missed the use of the term "dear." She looked from Nelly to Jason, a question on her face.

"I'm sure you remember Jason Miller," Nelly said as if they had not all known each other since childhood. "My husband now," she went on, stepping close and squeezing Jason's hand. He grinned weakly, torment in his eyes. Mother Maridem save us, Adara thought. The boy just couldn't keep it in his pants any longer, I suppose.

She pasted a big grin on her face and said, "Congratulations, you two! What a surprise! I suppose Jason's going to help out here in the store with you and your mother, then?" Her apparent indifference seemed to have worked, for Nelly was looking a little mollified. She and Adara had been, if not exactly bosom buddies, reasonably friendly growing up together in the area around Pine Hill. Adara's frequent trips to deliver potions to the store had often put them in contact.

"Mama's decided to retire," Nelly admitted with a genuine smile. "It's hard for her to be on her feet for so many hours every day, and Jason's papa doesn't really need him at the mill. We're expecting a child early next year." Oh, that went far to explain it.

"Congratulations again," Adara said sincerely. "I hope all goes well for you."

Now that the dreaded Former Girlfriend had been met, and had gracefully accepted defeat, Nelly seemed willing for them to be friends again. "So what about you, Adara? Did you find the magus who sent the demons?" The fine quality of Adara's garb had not gone unnoticed. No one in Pine Hill would have been able to afford such a getup, even had such clothing been available to buy.

Adara smiled and launched into a condensed version of what she'd been up to since leaving Pine Hill in the spring. She didn't belabor the relationship between her and Ferdyn, only referring to him as a champion and mentor who'd taught her much. Boy, had he ever.

Jason's eyes were shining, no doubt imagining what it might be like to go off and have stupendous adventures – carrying off bushels of gold at the end of them. Sorry boyo, you missed your chance, Adara thought with a hint of regret. She doubted there would ever have been a big romance between her and the cute miller's son, but they might certainly have had some fun together.

Eventually Adara bought a ham, a wheel of cheese, some beans and flour, that woolen shawl, and a few other items she knew would be appreciated around the Selden cottage. She also got a sack to carry it all in. For Malika there were some tidbits of river fish preserved in oil, which she sniffed at suspiciously until Adara sent, "It's good, eat up!"

The young woman and her grounded semigryph picked up the trail leading east out of town. It was getting on toward the dinner hour, though it would be light out for another couple of hours at least. Not that Adara was worried about returning the two miles to town in darkness. There were no bears, wolves, or lions this close to town, and she could have walked the path blindfolded.

They detoured along the way for Malika to drink from a little rivulet that ran a few paces south of the path, and for the little semigryph to make an unsuccessful attempt at catching a squirrel. It quickly escaped into the upper branches of a pine tree, chittering angrily at her. "Not now," Adara sent, and her charge reluctantly backed down.

They arrived at the cottage beside the meadow to find young Ellie Forrest sitting on a stool in the front yard beside a bucket of steaming water, plucking a chicken for supper. She set the bird down and jumped to her feet. "Adara!" she cried, running to greet the young woman who'd become something of an idol to her. Adara had been granted a six-year head start in learning all Nanny had to teach, and it sometimes seemed to Ellie as if she would never catch up.

Malika immediately trotted over to sniff at the corpse of the bird, hunger rising. Adara had to send a strong prohibition with an edge of mastery to prevent her from making off with it. "To me!" she commanded mentally, and the semigryph reluctantly obeyed.

"Oh, a wildcat... ?" Ellie said, realizing that the creature was not quite the right shape. The ears were bigger, and it was a little huskier all over – especially in the chest.

"Malika's a semigryph," Adara explained, and the girl's eyes got wide.

"Can... can I pet her?" she asked hesitantly. She had never seen one of these rare animals before, but it certainly looked soft and fuzzy.

Malika had come to find that she enjoyed being stroked and petted, and after obtaining her permission silently Adara told Ellie, "Go ahead. She likes to be scratched behind the ears, but don't touch her in the area where the cloth is tied. She has a broken wing, and it still hurts a little."

Nanny, who'd been working in the cottage's kitchen, heard their voices and stepped out. Her face lit with joy at the sight of the adoptive daughter she'd feared she might never see again. Tears burning her eyes, Adara enfolded the old woman in a powerful hug, kissing her forehead. "Oh Nanny, it's so good to see you!" she murmured.

The old woman hugged her back with surprising strength. She might be nearly eighty years old, but she was one of the best healers in Rivermarch and she knew how to take care of herself. Nanny stepped back and looked Adara up and down. Then she looked down at the semigryph, who was sitting on her haunches with her head stretched up and her eyes closed, purring in enjoyment at Ellie's ministrations.

Nanny raised an eyebrow. "Looks like you've had yourself some adventures, dear," she remarked mildly. "Come on inside and we'll talk. And Ellie, that chicken's not plucking itself." Adara stepped inside and set her sack down on the kitchen table, wondering at how much smaller the cottage seemed than she remembered it. She seriously doubted she had grown any physically in the past three months. It was her view of the world that had expanded.

A couple of hours later, as dusk was creeping over the land, Adara and Malika made their way back along the forest trail toward town. She, Nanny, and Ellie had dined happily on chicken and dumplings, and they had been amazed at her tale. Again, she had not provided any details about the nature of her connection with Ferdyn. But she knew from the appraising look Nanny gave her that her adoptive mother had easily guessed at what had not been said.

The Loggers' Rest's common room was full of local lads when Adara returned, and rather than go right off to her lonely bed she let Malika into the room to sleep and went herself to buy a few rounds for the crowd. She knew most of these men, young and old, and they were eager to hear her tale of adventure. The fact that she was buying them all ales helped to back up the part of the story that involved the demons' treasure, but she could tell that several in her audience had their doubts. Nobody offered to accompany her to her bed, which was probably just as well. Adara might be willing to act like a slut, now that she'd developed a taste for sex; but she didn't want to be perceived as one here in the town she'd grown up in.

Chapter 5

Adara stayed in Pine Hill for two more days, visiting with old friends and spreading the tale of her adventures far and wide. Then she was ready to move on. After talking it over with Nanny, she had finally concluded that she was ready to visit Willoughby – the place where she had been born.

As soon as she'd recovered her earliest childhood memories, triggered by the sight of the dead demons outside Nanny's cottage, everyone had expected her to want to go back to Willoughby and learn what had truly happened. Did she not have an aunt and uncle there, her father's brother and his wife? But she had been reluctant to probe that old wound, and taking the fight to the demon bringer had seemed like a better course of action.

Now, she was out of excuses. According to the superior maps Adara had bought in Carlienne, Willoughby was a hundred miles upriver from Pine Hill. There were two other landmarks between them, a little mining town called Stonedon and a market village known as Sanders Mill.

It was a wonder, Adara thought, as she rode along the road overlooking the narrow canyon of the Willough to her left, that she had even survived that trip down to Pine Hill in her father's little fishing skiff. The first rapids had come as a shock and surprise, and the panicked six-year-old she'd been had dropped the last of her oars. By the time she had hit the second rapids, near Stonedon, she had been lying unconscious in the bottom of the boat and drifting at the whim of the current. It must surely have been Maridem's mercy that brought her to shore near Pine Hill before she had expired of hunger and thirst!

There was an inn in Stonedon, but Adara pushed on long past suppertime to stop for the night in Sanders Mill. Along the way she'd shot a rabbit from the saddle, and Malika was well-fed and asleep on the saddlebow as they made their way into town. The little semigryph would eat almost anything if Adara urged her to do so, but she knew fresh raw meat or fish would be much better for the creature and she tried to provide it when she could.

"It's late for supper," the innkeeper told her. He'd demanded that what he took to be a large cat be confined to the room, not liking its looks.

"I'll take whatever you've got," Adara assured him. She had snacked on trail bread, nuts, and dried fruit during the afternoon and early evening while riding along, but she longed for a real hot meal.

Her supper turned out to be scrambled eggs with bacon and buttered toast, unconventional but warm and filling. As she sat washing it down with some small beer, Adara looked around the common room. Sanders Mill made Pine Hill seem like a bustling metropolis, as the latter town had its lumbering industry to keep things moving along. But it was one of the few towns in this part of Rivermarch, and the inn did get travelers.

Those three lifting pints together over in the corner, Adara took to be locals – farmers, perhaps, drinking up some of the proceeds from the sale of whatever it was they'd brought to market. And the young man and woman sharing a small table were gazing into each other's eyes in a way that made her think they might be recent newlyweds. Mmm.

And then there was that dark fellow across the way. He looked to be in his early twenties, probably an inch or so shorter than Adara was, with dark brown hair and black eyes set off by a complexion as pale as her own. He was handsome in a somewhat sinister fashion, and dressed all in black. Intriguing…

They'd been stealing covert glances at each other since Adara had come in. Now their eyes met, and he gave a white-toothed grin and raised an eyebrow in question. May I join you?

Oh, why not? Adara beckoned with her beer mug, and he rose fluidly to his feet and walked over to sit in the other chair at her table. The man moved with a pantherine grace. Another adventurer, like Ferdyn?

Adara mentally chastised herself. Was she doomed, for the rest of her life, to compare every man she met to her former lover? Sigh, probably. "Good evening," he said, extending a hand. "I'm Stellan Archer. Might I ask your name?" Hmm, none of the smooth blandishments and overdone charm Ferdyn had used the first time they met… stop it!

25

"Adara Willoughby," she said, taking the hand and squeezing it firmly. One of those wing-like black brows rose.

"A local girl?" he asked.

"Sort-of local," she admitted. "I was born in Willoughby, but grew up in Pine Hill. And more recently, I've been living in Carlienne." She wanted to establish herself as a woman of the world, someone who knew a few things – not some country bumpkin.

"Ah, Carlienne!" Stellan replied. "One of my favorite cities, though Riparre is my birthplace." Being a native of Rivermarch's capital made him something of a city sophisticate – at least for this backwater duchy, Adara thought. Though Riparre, as cities went, was a far cry from Carlienne or even homely Grandwyl.

Noticing that Adara's beer was gone, Stellan suggested "Might we share a bottle of red wine? They have an excellent local vintage here."

"All right," she replied with a coy glance. This Stellan didn't look exactly… trustworthy, but she was already beginning to feel a strong attraction. Probably she'd just been too long without sex, she mused. But she had no local reputation to protect, here. Let's have some wine and see what happens.

After the wine had been served Adara asked, "So what brings you so far afield, Stellan?" He smiled deprecatingly, dark eyes flashing, and gestured with his glass.

"I'm an incurable wanderer, I'm afraid," he admitted. "I left my parents' household at sixteen and have been bouncing around Tanar ever since. When I encounter an economic opportunity, I take advantage of it. There's always someplace with a surfeit of goods, and someplace where those goods are sought after. It keeps me comfortably enough."

Now it was Adara's turn to lift an eyebrow. Stellan's tale rang a little hollow, somehow. "And what about you, Adara?" he asked. "What brings you to the bustling metropolis of Sanders Mill on this warm summer evening?" She smiled at him demurely.

"I'm going back in time," she explained. At his questioning look, she went on. "My parents were killed in an attack by demons around eleven years ago. I escaped and was taken in by an old lady in Pine Hill who raised me as her own. Long story short, I've finally worked up the courage to return to Willoughby and find out if I still have any relatives in that town."

"Demons?" Stellan asked. Oh, she was going to have to tell the entire story again. Dozens more times, no doubt.

"The Swinzen, pig-men from another dimension," Adara began, and her companion exclaimed "Them!" She goggled at him. Certainly no one in Pine Hill had known anything of the strange creatures. It was why she had gone to Carlienne seeking answers.

"I ran into a party of what I could only describe as 'pig-men' when I was traveling up in Leamarch a couple of months ago," the young man said. "There were five of them, a little shorter than the average man but very husky, with arms too long for their bodies and faces like swine – long snouts, tusks. Does that sound like these Swinzen you spoke of?"

"That's them," Adara said in astonishment. A couple of months ago? That was right around the time when all of Sarand Bloodspire's Swinzen troops, freed of his sorcerous control, had returned through the portal to their own world. Then she realized: Nanny had said there had been more, that day. She'd killed three and a fourth had fled, but it had returned with companions and they'd knocked her out before ransacking the cottage and fleeing again. They must have been trying to make their way back to Kragstein when they had suddenly found themselves cut adrift – free from the magus' powers, but lost in a world not their own.

"How did you come upon them?" Adara asked, her blue-eyed gaze pinned on her companion's face as she leaned slightly across the table.

He hesitated, then replied, "I was anxious to get someplace, and was traveling at night headed southeast. The five of them attacked me on the road, moving on foot. I thought they might have wanted to rob me of my horses."

"And...?" Adara asked. Had he just ridden them down, leaving the troop roaming free within Tanar?

"I was forced to kill them, I'm afraid," Stellan replied. "They were armed with swords and axes, and dressed in studded leather armor. But they didn't really seem to be all that competent as fighters. They kept getting in each other's way."

27

The girl was looking at him, not with the awe he'd half expected after reporting he'd mown down five antagonists single-handed, but rather with cool appraisal. Who *was* this enchanting creature? It seemed clear to Stellan that there was a lot more to her than met the eye. And was that *irilium* plate studding her vest? He just *had* to get to know her better.

"They injured my horse trying to get at me with their swords," Stellan went on. "I camped there by the side of the road until it was light enough for me to see, then patched him up and I was on my way again. But I got a really good look at my antagonists before I left. They had on livery, with a staring eye above a terzidrac on their surcoats."

"That was the arms of Sarand Bloodspire, the Mancer King," Adara said matter-of-factly. She launched once more into her tale, skipping most of the preliminaries and describing how she and her companion had taken down the evil magus, freed the people under his thrall, banished the Swinzen back to their home dimension, and walked away with an "adequate reward." No way did she intend to tell this chance-met stranger that she was carrying a small fortune in gold secreted amidst her belongings – or that those coins were only a small portion of her net worth.

The bottle of wine was almost done, and both of them were feeling pretty mellow. A genuine smile curved Stellan's lips as he said, "An amazing tale, Adara! I suppose that accounts for your rather... *unique* vest. And what do you plan to do after you've revisited the old sod? Any new adventures planned?"

Adara gave him a lazy grin, her eyes half-lidded. "I'm young yet," she replied sweetly, "and the world offers many possibilities. But I thought I might try my hand at some... archaeological investigations. So much of pre-Unification history has been lost or muddled. Even within a few days travel of Willoughby there are several legendary sites worthy of exploration. Who knows what ancient mysteries I might solve?"

Stellan's eyes lit, the intrigue within them clear. "I'm very interested in old legends and ancient ruins myself," he said, looking into her eyes. "And it happens I'm at loose ends for the moment.

Might you be interested in a partner on this expedition of yours? Somebody to help you excavate, watch your back, and so forth?"

Somebody who just happens to be capable of killing five Swinzen soldiers in a night fight? Adara thought. Why, yes... Adara seriously doubted it was the chances for scholarly discovery that appealed to Stellan, however. "I must warn you," she said, "there is a likelihood that my investigations might not yield any plunder. I'm truly more interested in learning about the ancients than in stripping their tombs of valuables. Perhaps, rather than a partnership, I could hire you to come along and help?"

He looked at her questioningly, and Adara went on. "I'd pay for all the food and equipment. I assume you have a horse or horses of your own, so you provide your own mount. You help with any digging or fighting that's required, and assist with taking care of the horses, setting up camp, cooking meals, and so forth. I pay you two marks per week, and should we happen to come away from our expedition with any... souvenirs, you'll share in them. Does that sound like something you'd be interested in doing? I suppose if you're used to being your own boss..."

"No, that would be fine!" Stellan broke in. His mind was already pondering the possibilities. And one of those calculations was, did his prospective employer have a policy against fraternization? "When will you start out on this expedition?"

Adara grinned at him again, suddenly looking much younger than she had a couple of minutes ago. How old was she, anyway? Stellan didn't recall her saying. Indeed, other than the bare facts of her and this "companion" of hers triumphing over the demon bringer, her story hadn't offered all that much detail.

"I'm leaving for Willoughby in the morning," she told him. "Getting it over with once and for all. I might have an aunt and uncle still living there, and if so I should be able to find out from them what went on in town after my parents were killed and I went missing. I might need to stay there for a couple of days, but then I plan to head straight north up into the Ratskells. It should be possible to ford the river near Willoughby."

"Oh, we won't need to ford it," Stellan assured her. "There's a bridge at Willoughby now, built around six years ago. Old Duke

Zoltan collaborated with the Duke of Northmarch, who supplied the stone. They hoped it would open up more trade between the two duchies, and it has to some extent. If you haven't been to Willoughby in eleven years, I think you're going to be surprised."

"Well, I suppose if you just meet me in Willoughby, say in the public market square at noon two days hence, I might be finished with my business by then," Adara said.

"Don't be silly," Stellan replied. "Meet me right here tomorrow morning for breakfast, and we'll go to Willoughby together. I don't mind hanging out there for a few days, in fact I wouldn't mind meeting your relatives if you've got any."

With that the young man downed the last of his wine and got to his feet. He took Adara's right hand and brought it to his lips, a hint of mischief in his eyes. "Good night, boss," he said cheerfully. "See you in the morning."

Chapter 6

That night Adara brought herself to orgasm as Malika slept at the foot of the bed, oblivious to the disturbance. She had found meeting Stellan to be both exciting and a little disturbing. Could he really be trusted? Ah, but what did she have to fear? With Voleur, her dagger, and her irilium plate armor, she herself could probably cut her way through half a dozen Swinzen soldiers without breaking a sweat. And there were always the elementals to call to her aid. She hoped, though, that he would not prove to be a rotter of some stripe. She was starting to make some plans for that mysterious young man.

Adara wore her leathers again today, though it was only another thirty miles or so to Willoughby and the area seemed fairly civilized. Before going in to breakfast she got her pack wrapped up, Voleur in its harness leaning against it, and let Malika out the window. The entire inn was on one floor. "Stay close," she warned silently, and the semigryph crept silently down toward the river's edge. She'd spotted a couple of crows picking at the carcass of a very dead salmon; and while her kind was far too fastidious to eat carrion unless starving, the idea of some fresh crow seemed appealing.

Following Malika's progress with half her mind while she made her way to the common room, Adara mused on the situation with her furry friend. How was having a convalescent wild animal along with her going to fit into her plans? She ought just to have hardened her heart and left the kit to die, broken and half-drowned on the riverbank. But now she was determined that Malika should live – grow strong, grow up, and return to the life she was meant to have.

Stellan was already seated at the same table they'd shared last night, looking bright-eyed and bushy-tailed. And quite tasty, actually. His chin was freshly shaven, his dark hair glossy and tied back with a length of red ribbon. And he'd doffed the black garb in favor of a sort of forester's costume – dark green hose, soft brown boots, brown leather doublet. Like her vest, the doublet seemed to have something of armor about it.

Adara smiled happily at him and sat down. "I had breakfast for dinner last night," she remarked. "I wonder if they'll serve me beef stew to break my fast with." Stellan shook his head, laughter glinting in his black eyes, and gestured toward the bar. A serving maid was approaching them with a tray piled high with breakfast goodies.

"I took the liberty of ordering for us," he said. "I hope you don't mind..." Adara's eyes widened as she saw freshly baked pastries, summer fruits, and bowls of oatmeal – studded with raisins, and swimming in butter and cream with a dollop of honey. Mmm!

"Thank you, this'sh wonnerful!" she said around a mouthful of pastry. She and Ferdyn had been eating quite well in Carlienne of course, and not having to cook any of it themselves. But during her weeks on the road coming here, Adara had often been on short commons. Her mouth full of warm goodness, she let her mind drift out to find Malika – and was surprised and delighted to discover the little semigryph spitting out a mouthful of black feathers as she savaged the corpse of the crow she'd killed. Aw, my baby is growing up...

They washed their breakfast down with warm tea. In Carlienne Adara had discovered another way to obtain her dose of motherwort – the dried leaves ground to a fine powder, which could then be sprinkled over one's food or even downed with a swallow of water. Though she'd been without a lover for weeks, she'd kept up the regimen – wanting to be ready if any opportunities came up. Ah, ever hopeful.

Adara produced a pinch of the powder and sprinkled it over half a fresh peach, before devouring it in a few bites. She looked up to see Stellan watching her thoughtfully. The corners of his mouth quirked up ever so slightly, and she blushed. But she covered her discomfort by washing down the fruit with another swig of tea. Then she stood up, brushing crumbs from her lap.

"Time to go," she said briskly. "Meet you in the stableyard?" Stellan nodded cheerfully, and a few minutes later the boy had finished tying her pack and other items to Sadiq's back, saddling Zarhya. Stellan emerged from the inn's rear door, carrying a much smaller pack. He wore a sword at his hip, a little shorter than Voleur. On the other hip was a long dagger.

As they waited for his tall bay gelding to be saddled, the pack tied behind the saddle, Stellan eyed Voleur's hilt standing over Adara's right shoulder and raised an eyebrow. "You know how to use that?" he asked casually. She nodded. "Did you take off the Mancer King's head, then?"

"Nope, I poisoned him," Adara replied as casually. "He was expecting to rape me at the time, so I figured it was fair."

Involuntarily, Stellan took half a step away. Any thoughts he might have harbored about getting into his new employer's bed by main force had just vanished – not that he was a rapist, in any case. He turned his attention to Adara's horses. "Very nice," he said, gesturing at Zarhya where she stood – tall and alert and graceful. Adara smiled. She'd become very fond of the mare over the months since buying her.

"She's a great horse," Adara said with enthusiasm. "And old Sadiq's not bad either." With the other part of her mind, she was following Malika's progress. She had finished bathing herself after literally eating crow, and was now on her way to join them.

Stellan started back, muttering an oath, as the semigryph launched herself between them and up onto Zarhya's saddle. "*There's* my sweetie!" Adara cried, walking over to pet Malika's head and scratch her behind the ears as the kit purred and kneaded the saddle with those wicked front talons.

"That's a semigryph!" Stellan gasped, astonished. So far as he knew, no one had ever tamed such a creature. "But what's the matter with her wings?" he went on, curiosity piqued.

"She's just a kit," Adara explained, telling how she'd found Malika on the road and was nursing her back to health. She didn't mention her ability to see through the semigryph's eyes, or communicate silently with the little creature. Until she knew Stellan better, she saw no reason to reveal too many secrets.

Shaking his head but smiling inside, Stellan climbed aboard his gelding and the little party set off along the road east. "He's a pretty boy," Adara said of the nearly black horse. "What's his name?"

"Zoli," Stellan said with a sly grin. "I named him after our illustrious duke. Do you not see the resemblance?" Adara chuckled, though she had never seen so much as a picture of Duke Zoltan of Rivermarch and would not have known him if he'd come up and asked her for directions.

"He and Zarhya make a nice couple," Adara suggested as they rode along. The dapple gray mare was pale, the gelding dark, and from Zoli's heavier build he was no Khoureshi. She was just being whimsical. Soon their conversation turned to other things.

Once again Adara found herself comparing her new companion to Ferdyn. It was inevitable, she supposed. Where Ferdyn had been ebulliently charming, dashing, fun-loving, and open, Stellan was friendly and cheerful enough – but reserved. She found herself drawn to him by his air of mystery, as if he were a puzzle she longed to solve.

"Do you have family, Stellan?" Adara asked casually. Her question was disguised as small talk, but she really wanted to learn more about this enigmatic young man – before she trusted him as a companion on an expedition that might prove perilous. He rode with a bow at his side just as she did, and even in his less-severe forester garb he had an air of danger about him. Do *I*, she wondered as they rode along? She definitely *was* dangerous, but that wasn't how she thought of herself.

"Plenty of it," he remarked with an edge of facetiousness. "Mother, Father, a few aunts and uncles, a couple of grandparents..." Adara eyed him thoughtfully, and he continued. "I have two older brothers, and a couple of sisters."

"You're the baby of the family?" she asked. Having been an only child and orphaned at a young age, being surrounded by a pack of relations was like a foreign country – though one she'd visited for a time when she and Ferdyn had been together.

Stellan gave her a wry smile, dark eyes flashing amusement. "Not the baby, no," he said. "More like the black sheep. The last time I spoke with Father, he strongly suggested I should not darken their door ever again." Really! How intriguing. Just *how* bad a boy was Stellan, anyhow? Would he steal her purse? Her horse? Or perhaps, her heart?

The morning was warm and pleasant, and they rode along together talking of this and that as the miles rolled away beneath the horses' hooves. This far east, the wedge-shaped peninsula that constituted Rivermarch rose gently toward the south and there were many farmsteads in view. No wilderness here, as existed between

Pine Hill and the Willough Bridge, and they were scarcely paying attention to their surroundings. It was unlikely any gang of bandits would haunt *this* stretch of the river road.

They climbed down from the horses at midday, still a few miles short of Willoughby, and picnicked under an oak tree beside the road as Zarhya, Sadiq, and Zoli cropped the nearby grasses and Malika went exploring in a copse of willows down near the riverside. Flushed from her success with the crow this morning, she returned to Adara carrying the bleeding corpse of a water rat.

Adara was just polishing off the last of the sandwiches the innkeeper had packed for them, and recoiled in distaste at this offering. "All yours," she sent silently to the semigryph, and Malika happily dropped to the ground beside the humans and began dismantling her prey with relish.

"Your little friend seems to be turning into quite the hunter," Stellan remarked, dusting the crumbs from his thighs as he got onto his feet and took a long pull from a water skin.

"It's surprising," Adara admitted. "I'm not exactly an expert on semigryphs, but I thought they usually didn't develop their hunting skills until they're full grown."

"Might be the fact that she's grounded," he suggested. "Learning how to hunt from the air must take a lot more skill and practice, and the kits would ordinarily not be hunting on the ground until they were fully fledged." What a thought, Adara mused. Likely he was right.

"Well, we're almost there," she said with a sigh. "Better get on with it."

Less than an hour later, the terrain on either side of the road was beginning to look familiar to Adara. She recognized that low bluff on the north side of the river. Somewhere not far to the east of here should be the house... There! But it was no snug cottage she saw, a few dozen yards to the south of where the pilings of a ruined jetty stood forlornly in the shallows at the river's edge. A stone chimney, partially collapsed, stood amid the remnants of stone foundations. The house had burned!

Pulling Zarhya up and hopping down out of the saddle with a murmured command to stay, Adara walked slowly toward the sad ruins of her childhood home. Malika scampered beside her, and Stellan got down to join her as she stared at smoke-smudged stones, little bits of charcoal in among the dirt enclosed by the foundation.

Stellan glanced over at Adara. She overtopped him by a small amount, but they were nearly eye to eye. And hers were filling up with tears. Head down, Adara stifled a sob. From the moment she had reclaimed her early memories, she had known, had accepted that her mama and papa were dead. And the knowledge hadn't bothered her that much. She had a warm and loving home with Nanny Selden, and they had always supposed that she was probably an orphan. Why, now, did the sight of this pathetic ruin hit her so hard emotionally?

Angrily swiping an arm over her eyes and shaking her head, Adara blinked and began stalking around the perimeter of the place in her tall boots. Mama had kept a kitchen garden out back there, adding vegetables to the fish and game that made up most of their meals. Over there was the big dead stump where she'd played fanciful games with her imaginary friends. Living three miles out from town, little Adara had had few playmates.

And there, off to the west of the barely-discernible area that had once been dug up for planting beans and cabbages, was a weathered wooden plank stuck into the ground. The top had been carved into a circle, the symbol of Father Baldor, and a single word was carved beneath: "Willoughby." With an inarticulate cry, Adara fell to her knees atop the grave and began sobbing. Stellan knelt beside her and gathered her in his arms, just letting her cry out her long-postponed grief.

36

Chapter 7

After Adara had pulled herself together, disentangling herself from Stellan with a murmur of thanks, she dusted herself off and they continued up the road into Willoughby. The old family homestead was no longer three miles from town, they found. Long before reaching what in Adara's dim childhood memories were the outskirts of the village, they began encountering cottages, smallholdings, and even the occasional business. And ahead in the distance, Adara could see a fine granite bridge spanning the river in two tall arches. Amazing!

"You're right, Stellan," she told her companion. "I can't believe how much this place has grown – it was nothing but a market and fishing village eleven years ago." He nodded, smiling. "Where next?" he asked. "How will you attempt to find your uncle and aunt?"

They had come to a broad waterfront plaza that gave off the river road perhaps two hundred yards west of the new bridge. Off to the south, Willoughby's main street ran up a slight slope toward a new, stone-paved market square. Adara gestured in that direction. "I was thinking of taking rooms at an inn, and then going out into town on foot and asking around the marketplace. If my particular branch of the Willoughby family still lives around here, likely some of the merchants will know of them."

"A very sensible scheme," Stellan replied. "There's an inn right over there." When Adara had been born the village of Willoughby had boasted but a single inn, a timber-built, two-storey affair not far from the river and called, prosaically, the River Inn. On rare visits to town, the little girl had once or twice been treated to lunch and sweetmeats there.

The old River Inn still stood, Adara saw. But the establishment Stellan pointed to was something else altogether. An imposing three-storey structure, it appeared to be built of the same gray stone as the new bridge – and was probably no older. Wow, she thought, and made a beeline for what eight-foot signs on two corners of the building proclaimed to be "The Willoughby Hotel."

This was a fairly recent style of hostelry beginning to be seen in cities around Tanar. Like the Duke's Head in Grandwyl, these establishments usually offered their clientele services beyond the simple bed, board, and drink provided by most old-time inns. Their room rates reflected their amenities, so places like the River Inn were in no danger of being put out of business anytime soon; but Adara could scarcely believe that sleepy little Willoughby held such a thing.

There was a gated, fenced yard around the side nearest the river, and they went in that way to leave off the horses. A problem immediately arose concerning Malika. Dogs and other pets were not permitted on the premises. "She's just my pet wildcat," Adara protested. "Can't she stay in the barn with the horses? She'll earn her keep catching rats…"

At Adara's silent suggestion, the semigryph had hopped down from the saddle and vanished up into the hayloft where fodder for the clients' horses was stored, as soon as the stableman's objections had been voiced. She returned a couple of minutes later, as the horses were being unloaded, with a rat dangling limply from her jaws and what looked a lot like a grin on her furry face.

"Oh, all right," the stableman said. "As long as she doesn't cause any trouble with the horses." Predators the size of a semigryph didn't trigger panic in horses the way a whiff of their larger cousins might. And Adara was in almost constant mental communication with Malika – ready to override her instincts if she stepped out of line.

A couple of young men in what looked like livery showed up to haul their luggage inside, and Adara and Stellan exchanged a glance. "Looks like this might just be the most expensive place in town," he remarked. "Are you buying?"

"Sure," Adara said cheerfully. "As long as you're on the payroll, I'll take care of your living expenses. But I expect you to help out with whatever I'm doing, too."

"Shall I go out and ask around about Willoughbys?" he asked, as they went in through the hotel's surprisingly grand carriage entrance. Adara snorted.

"Half the people in town call themselves Willoughby, and likely only a couple of them are actually my relatives," she said. The new style in Tanar, of taking surnames and keeping them from generation to generation, had only gotten underway a couple of centuries earlier and most families were still named for their occupation or the town they hailed from.

They had arrived in a broad, airy room with glass windows looking out on the main street, and a long desk running along the back wall. Another young man in the same livery as the two carrying their luggage stood behind it, a large ledger book in front of him. He looked up and smiled as they and their entourage appeared.

Of course it was Stellan he addressed. While women might be found in many walks of life within the kingdom of Tanar, when a man and a woman were together it was customary to assume that he was in charge. "Good afternoon sir," the desk clerk said pleasantly. "A room for you and your…" He trailed off. Adara did not much resemble anyone's idea of a goodwife.

Stellan smiled and shrugged, and gestured for Adara to take over. "Two rooms, if you please," she said with a satisfied smile. "You have laundry service?"

"Of course, miss," the clerk said. "And if you wish your shoes or boots polished, just leave them outside the door. How many days will you be staying, if I may ask?"

Adara considered. If it turned out her uncle and his wife had moved away or died (the latter not likely, as they'd been little older than her father and should now still be under forty), it would still take her at least a day to outfit their expedition. She was quite pleased to see how Willoughby had grown, for it meant obtaining the supplies she wanted would be much easier. "Tonight and tomorrow night, for certain," she replied. "Should we need to stay for any additional nights I'll let you know."

"Very well," he said with a little smile. These two might look a little rough, but Adara's attitude had convinced him she was the sort of person who could afford to stay here. "I can put you side by side on the second floor, rooms 211 and 213, if that will be satisfactory. The rooms have windows overlooking the river."

Adara grinned broadly at him. "That'll be just fine," she said. So far money had not been discussed, and she now pulled out the heavy purse at her side. It was one of the many places she was keeping money, on this trip. Branches of the Royal Bank of Tanar were spread thinly in this part of the kingdom, and she hoped she would not run short of cash.

"Oh, there's no need to pay now," the clerk told her. "Anything you need while you're here, meals in the dining room or other extras, can be added to your bill." He took down their names, and Adara signed a form stating she was liable for all the charges. She wondered just how heart-stopping that bill was going to be.

One more thing… "I would like to have a bath. Can you provide one in the room?" Adara asked the clerk.

"We have private bathrooms on the first floor, down the hall," he replied with a gesture. "At this hour there should be no waiting." Well I'll be, Adara thought. So much for that brief, fluttering thought of inviting Stellan into the tub with her for some fun and games. Eh, it had only been a thought.

After getting ensconced in her room, which was spacious and well appointed, Adara changed into a garment that somewhat resembled the style of robe favored by sorcerers. But rather than being black with mystical symbols embroidered on it, it was the color of a summer sky with little seed pearls studding it across the front above the silken rope belt. Locking up and slipping the room key into her pocket, she stepped next door and tapped on the door of Stellan's room. He had raised no objections whatsoever to their separate accommodations, making her wonder – was he anywhere near as attracted to her as she was to him?

The door shortly opened, and she gaped to see him standing there in nothing but his hose – evidently caught in the midst of changing his clothes. He was quite well-muscled, but lean where Ferdyn had been bulky – a stag to Ferdyn's bull. He had a goodly patch of dark hair thatching his chest and running down his belly, but elsewhere the skin was pale and smooth – a few shades lighter than his face and hands.

Adara made an effort to close her mouth as her glance ran up from Stellan's bare torso to his face, and she realized that he was looking her over as appreciatively. Hmm, that answers *that* question, she thought. So far he had only seen her in her traveling clothes, dark hair pulled back in a ponytail. She looked considerably more like a woman in this garb, and as her glance traveled unbidden down his body once again she saw that the bulge in his hose had increased in size.

Stifling the grin that threatened to break out across her face, Adara said "Oh, sorry to bother you. I just wanted to let you know I'm going to go take a quick bath. Then I'll change into some town clothes and we can go out looking for Uncle Beldan and Aunt Olivia. All right?"

His warm smile and glinting dark eyes told her he knew exactly what she'd been thinking, and he liked it. "I was just about to go down for a bath myself," he said. "Wait just a moment, and I'll put on a robe." He made to close the door on her, then peered out through it and wiggled his eyebrows. "Unless you'd care to come inside while I change?"

Adara blushed, and grinned back. "Thanks, I'll wait here," she said chuckling. Inside, a thrill had started in her crotch and run right up through her core. Damn, it had been too long! Clearly a lack of cock in her life was starting to affect her judgment.

Less than a minute later Stellan appeared in a voluminous, floor-length wrap robe with a tie belt. It was black, of course, and had no ornamentation. "You remind me of a magus in that getup," Adara remarked as they made their way along the corridor and down the stairs. "You do any magic?" Another attempt to get more information about him, deflected as deftly as had been most of her others.

"I've dabbled," he said casually. "Little spells for lighting fires, things like that. But I'm certainly not what you'd call a magus." The subject was dismissed as they arrived at the entrance to the bathrooms. A young woman sat at a desk, and she handed each of them a bathroom key and a couple of thick towels. "Soap is in the rooms," she told them. "Can I offer you any scented salts, or liquid shampoo?" Stellan declined, but Adara decided to treat herself to both. Few aspects of being filthy rich gave her more pleasure than finding things to spend money on that seemed eminently worthwhile and not just a profligate waste of resources.

The two of them exchanged an appraising glance as they parted in the hallway, Adara to a room on the left as Stellan went to one on the right. Down the hall, a team of maidservants was clearing out a room and readying it for the next customer.

To Adara's astonishment the rooms actually had hot water coming out of pipes in the wall. The large freestanding copper tub had been freshly scrubbed after use by its last occupant, and by opening a valve as directed by a sign on the wall she soon had it filling with hot, steaming water. These baths must use the same hot water source as the hotel's laundry did, she guessed. There was a smaller pipe delivering room temperature water, and she added a little of that (along with a little of the scented bath salts) to the tub before climbing inside and lying back. Ahh, wonderful!

A longer time later than she'd anticipated, Adara emerged from the bathroom clad in her robe again. Her hair was clean, damp, and smelled faintly of roses. Stellan, who'd apparently been out of the bath for some time already, was lounging against the wall at the end of the corridor and chatting up the bath girl. The cad!

As soon as she came down the corridor toward them, though, his attention went immediately to her. He smiled broadly, eyes flashing in appreciation, and said softly "You look relaxed…" Oh, not as much as I'd be in an hour if you'd just come up to my room and relieve me of this little problem, Adara thought. But no, she must be good. She was here in Willoughby to look for her relatives and outfit her expedition, not hop into bed with handsome strangers.

Half an hour after that the two were dressed in clean clothing and walking up the rise from the hotel to Willoughby's central market square. Adara had donned an exquisitely fine but cool and lightweight cotton frock with a full skirt and snug, low-cut bodice that showed off her charms – such as they were – to best advantage. Like the robe, it was in a medium sky blue color that set off her eyes, creamy lace spilling out at the sleeves, neckline, and in a gore down the front of the skirt. Stellan's eyes had widened at the sight of her when he'd emerged from his own room a few minutes before.

Stellan, dressed in snug-fitting black pants and a black vest that left his muscular arms bare, looked like some kind of Gitano – those dark wanderers of Tanar's southern duchies. Considering his dark hair and eyes, perhaps there was some Gitano in his heritage, Adara mused.

This was not a market day, but Willoughby's market square was ringed with permanently-constructed stalls that were occupied daily, whenever weather permitted, by local merchants. Some of these merchants probably had regular shops housed in some of the nearby buildings, Adara guessed, but the extra visibility provided by the stalls probably brought them a lot of business.

"Why don't you go right and I'll go left," Adara suggested to Stellan, "and we'll meet over there on the far side of the square." He smiled.

"Sounds like a plan. I'm looking for a Beldan or Olivia Willoughby?"

"Or their son, my cousin Jeram," she replied. "He's a couple of years older than I am."

They parted, each making the rounds of the stands on one side of the square. Adara had an eye out for anything she might need on their expedition, as well. And for any familiar faces. Eleven years was a long time to her, but to someone who'd been an adult when she was a child it wasn't all that much. She might surely recognize some of the vendors who'd sold her parents goods while she was along, back then?

On the market square's west side, Stellan was making faster progress. He didn't intend to buy anything for the expedition, as Adara had said she was covering that. And while he'd been in Willoughby a few times in the five years since leaving Riparre, he had no acquaintances among its mercantile community.

So, he just made his way along from booth to booth. "Good afternoon, I'm wondering if you might know the whereabouts of Beldan, Olivia, or Jeram Willoughby? I've been instructed to deliver payment of a debt to Mister Willoughby or his family." He'd found that, if you were seeking someone, you were more likely to be given directions if the people you asked thought you meant to give that person money.

The answers ranged from "Sorry, don't know them," to "Thought I saw her a couple of weeks ago, don't know where they live though." But that was hopeful. At least, it seemed likely, Adara's aunt was still in the area. He came to a large stall that looked as though it was offering farm produce, though most of the others seemed to specialize in manufactured goods. And he was momentarily struck dumb.

The woman operating the stand, helped by a young adolescent boy and a girl of around nine, was tall and slender. She looked to be in her middle thirties, with a few laugh lines around her eyes, but still pretty – with that long, silky black hair and those big blue eyes... Stellan gaped at her, glanced across the square to where Adara was talking with the proprietor of a pottery stand, then back again.

"Excuse me, mistress," he said hesitantly, "I'm looking for a Beldan Willoughby. Might you know him?" The woman's eyes widened, looking Stellan over from head to foot and apparently concluding he was untrustworthy.

"Why do you ask?" she said coolly.

"Um, I..." for the first time in years, Stellan lost his cool. "Pardon me, I'll be right back!" he declared, and bolted across the square to take Adara's arm.

She turned eagerly to him. "Did you find something out?" she asked hopefully.

"You said your aunt was married to your father's brother?" he demanded.

"That's right," Adara confirmed. "I think he was a couple of years older than my papa, and they were our only relatives here. I don't remember what he did for a living. When you're six, these things don't always register on you." Six! Stellan thought irrelevantly. That meant she was... only seventeen? Amazing!

"Come with me," he told her, leading toward the other side of the square. "I think I found your mother!"

Chapter 8

Adara stood stock still before the stall, gazing at the woman who looked like a twenty-years-older version of herself. Her face had gone white, her mouth open in disbelief. The woman, whose attention had turned to a paying customer after Stellan had run off, looked up in annoyance that transformed in seconds to disbelief.

"M-mama?" Adara said in a tiny voice. Getting no response but a blank stare, she added "Elana Willoughby?" The stall keeper's eyes rolled up, and she fainted dead away. The little girl screamed and rushed to her mother's side, glaring up at the intruders.

"What did you do?" she demanded angrily. The boy, who looked around twelve and didn't bear much resemblance to his mother, peered hard at Adara and then knelt on the stone pavement. The woman was already coming around.

Meanwhile Adara had recovered herself and walked around to the rear so she could slip into the stall. Stellan just stood there bemused. Not so orphaned as all that, Adara, he thought triumphantly. The older woman got unsteadily to her feet as her little daughter clung to her skirts and her elder daughter stood gazing into her face. They were of a height. Tears of joy ran down Elana's face as she seized Adara in a tight hug. Almost in unison, they cried "I thought you were dead!"

Adara had gotten more than just her looks from her mother, Stellan soon realized. The steel that ran through that young woman was evident in Elana's spine as she quickly pulled herself together. "Jaime, start getting ready to close down," she commanded her son. Squeezing Adara's hand, she said. "We need to talk, but first I need to close up the stand. Oh, I can't really believe you're alive!" She hugged her again and bent to the work of stowing the goods on display in locked cabinets before closing the stall up tight for the evening.

Half an hour later the five of them were enjoying afternoon tea in the elegant dining room of the Willoughby Hotel. Unlike the dark, atmospheric common rooms of most of the inns across Tanar, this place was brightly lit, with a row of glass windows looking out on the main road. It seemed a more suitable place to bring children, though Elana had quailed at the expense until Adara had assured her that it was her treat.

"I was unconscious until the morning after the attack," Elana was telling her rapt audience. Neither Jaime nor his half-sister Leana had heard the full story before, and they were as intrigued as Adara and Stellan were. "I don't even remember dragging myself out of the house, but I must have. We were so isolated out there, no one came to see. The house was nothing but ashes by the time I came to, no longer smoking, and you and your father were gone. I stumbled into town and was taken in by Beldan and Olivia."

Adara was sitting beside her long-lost mother, and gave her hand a squeeze. "I didn't remember anything about my former life after I came to in Nanny Selden's cottage in Pine Hill," she supplied. "It wasn't until more of the Swinzen, those pig-men, came looking for me there that I was able to break through the trauma and recover all the memories I'd lost."

"They were looking for you?" Elana asked, searching her daughter's face. Adara nodded and gestured to her throat, with a sidewise glance at Stellan. She wasn't eager to have him learn about the Darkshield just yet. Though it occurred to her that if she did, as she rather hoped, get naked with him pretty soon, it was a topic that was bound to come up.

Adara told Elana of growing up in Pine Hill with Nanny Selden, learning the herbal arts (about which she had not yet told Stellan, and he was intrigued). "But when you had reclaimed your memories, why did you not return here?" her mother asked, hurt.

"I knew the demons were after me, and twice they had attacked those I loved," Adara explained. "It seemed likely that anywhere I went, those creatures might come looking for me sooner or later. Nanny had killed three of them during their attack at her cottage, and I had cut the device from one's surcoat. It seemed to me that the only thing for me to do was learn who was sending the demons, and put a stop to them once and for all."

Elana looked at her daughter wide-eyed. This Nanny Selden, to whom she was grateful for rescuing and raising the daughter she had thought lost forever, sounded like a very formidable person. And she seemed to have raised Adara to be the same.

For the umpteenth time in the last couple of months, Adara told the entire tale of her quest to Carlienne for answers – followed by the trek to Kragstein and the eventual downfall of the Mancer King. Mindful of her audience – which included her mother, two children, and a man she was hoping to hook up with – Ferdyn got *extremely* short shrift in this version. "Oh, I had enlisted some help…" was about the extent of it.

"So, you remarried?" Adara asked, glancing at the children. The boy was too old, surely, to be her brother – unless maybe Mama had been pregnant at the time of the attack. Like the girl, he had medium brown hair – though his eyes were brown, his sister's hazel.

Elana flushed slightly, though there was no accusation in Adara's tone. She had been a young woman in her middle twenties, a widow, her only child gone and presumed killed by a troop of armed monstrosities. What was she supposed to do – mourn forever?

"About a year after the… incident," she began, "I was still living with Beldan and Olivia, of course, and being in the bosom of their family with young Jeram was a great comfort to me. But I met Joseph at the shop. You might not know, your aunt and uncle run a dry goods store in town. It's around four blocks from here. Anyhow, Jaime's mother had died birthing him. Joseph was a young widower with a baby son, and I was a widow. We just sort of… gravitated to each other, you might say. We were married a few months later."

Adara smiled warmly and gave her mother a little hug. "I'm so glad you were able to find happiness," she said – meaning it. "So this is Jaime, and…"

"Your little sister is Leana," her mother said. "Leana Underhill." Adara solemnly shook hands with each of the children, her eyes sparkling.

"Pleased to meet you, brother, sister." They smiled shyly at her. After hearing the story of Adara's quest, Jaime had already decided that this big sister who had materialized in his life was the most exciting thing he could ever remember happening in Willoughby.

"You're farmers?" Adara asked.

Her mother nodded, but said "More or less. Joseph inherited a large sheep and cattle ranch with truck farm operation that his family had built up over the generations. The house is more like a country chateau than a farmhouse. The kids and I like to come into town a couple of days a week and operate the stand, just for a little pocket money and to have a chance to visit with friends in town. Joseph manages the place, and does all the paperwork. But we have hands doing all the real farm work." She picked up her teacup, pinky extended, and said with a roll of her eyes, "I'm very nearly a lady, at least in these parts."

Adara and Stellan both grinned at that. The two women were alike in so many ways, he thought wonderingly. Though so far at least, their paths in life had been very different. They all finished their tea, Adara signed for the charges to be added to her hotel bill, and they made their way back out into the afternoon sunshine.

"I cut your sales day short," Adara remarked ruefully.

"It's not a problem, Leana declared. "Nothing we brought with us won't keep until later on in the week. Come on, I'm going to take you to meet your aunt and uncle. They should both still be on duty at Willoughby Mercantile at this hour."

The family store proved to be the entire ground floor of a good-sized two-storey wooden building, just a block off of the main road and two blocks south of the market square. The once-placid village continued on up the gentle slope for several more blocks, gradually spreading to the east and west. Uncle Beldan and Aunt Olivia lived in a large apartment above the store, though Jeram – now nineteen – was living in the quarters of the carpentry shop where he'd apprenticed and was now a journeyman.

Another Willoughby enterprise closed early that day, as the excited Beldan and Olivia welcomed their long-lost niece back to the fold. They locked up the store and everyone adjourned upstairs. Stellan was beginning to feel a little like a fifth wheel, surrounded by Adara's relations. He hadn't much missed hobnobbing with any of his *own* family, in the years since his disgrace. But he bore it with equanimity. It was an amazing thing for the orphaned young woman to discover all these people who loved her, and who was he to cast a pall on the gathering by being impatient to leave?

As evening was coming on Leana excused herself and the children. "We must be getting back to Underhill," she said regretfully. "Cook will be expecting us for supper." They had brought a wagon into town, and left it in the Willoughbys' carriage house for the day as was their usual habit when coming to sell fleeces, hides, cheeses, and other goods at their marketplace stand.

Adara and Stellan were given careful instructions on reaching Underhill, which stood some four miles southeast of town. "We'll see you tomorrow when you get there," Leana told them firmly. "Joseph will be so excited when I tell him the news! And if you'd like, you can check out of the hotel and come stay with us. There are at least four unused bedrooms in the house, and we'd love to have you." She hugged and kissed Adara, and even hugged Stellan and planted a kiss on his cheek. She might have thought him a suspicious-looking stranger on first glance, but it was he who had brought her beloved daughter home to her at last.

Olivia insisted that they stay for supper, preparing a delicious hot pot with local vegetables and some lamb she said had come from Underhill. "Your mother makes sure we never lack for meat," she told Adara. "Though without Jeram here to eat it we don't get through much."

"I'd love to see Jeram, too," Adara said as they were sitting down to the hot and hearty bowlfuls of delicately-flavored stew.

Olivia smiled ruefully. She was a short, somewhat plump woman a little older than Elana, a few gray hairs barely visible on her dark blonde head. "If we can pry him away from Demelza Carpenter for an evening, we'll come out to Underhill while you're here and bring him along."

The hour was getting late as Adara kissed her aunt and uncle goodbye, thanking them for the meal, and went arm-in-arm with Stellan down the street toward their hotel. The group had drunk several bottles of a passable red wine with the meal, and both once again were feeling mellow.

After they had gotten back onto the main road they found their way lit by torches, hung on the sides of buildings at frequent intervals. It was almost like being in a city. "Oh, Stellan!" Adara gasped, as they strolled along in the warm summer evening. "All this family – it's almost too much for me to take in!" He put his arm around her waist and gave her an affectionate squeeze.

"Did you imagine it could be like this?" he asked softly. He certainly had not, else he might not have opted to join Adara from the beginning. His interest was in legendary tombs, plunder, and adventure – not sweet family gatherings. The Willoughbys and Adara's mother had been nice enough, certainly… but hour upon hour of that sort of thing was not his cup of tea.

On the other hand, all other things being equal, if he wanted to accompany Adara on this proposed expedition of discovery he would have had to hang around in Willoughby waiting until she was ready to leave, anyhow. At least this way he got to spend some more time in her oh-so-beguiling company.

When they got to their rooms, they stood in the hall facing each other. Adara wanted him, but her desire was muted by the emotional exhaustion of this unbelievable day – and those several glasses of wine, as well. "Adara," Stellan said softly, stepping close to murmur in her ear, "would you care to share my bed this night?"

She pulled away a little to look him in the eyes, black as pools of night in the dimly-lit corridor. She squeezed his hands. "I *would* care to share your bed, I think," she said softly. "But this night, I fear I am too tired to do you justice. There will be others." She stepped forward and kissed him, hard, on the mouth. In an instant his arms were around her, squeezing her tight, and his tongue slipped past her lips. They stood like that, locked together, for an endless moment. Then Adara pulled away, panting, and slipped through the door of her room and shut it behind her. With an aching in his loins, Stellan opened up his own door and went inside.

Chapter 9

"Things have come up, and as it happens I must leave today," Adara told the desk clerk in the morning. They'd had a delicious breakfast in the hotel dining room, but the invitation to stay at her relatives' "almost a country chateau" for free was too appealing. It was probably going to take her a few more years of being rich, she mused, before she really got into the spirit of the thing. After she saw – and paid – the bill, she *knew* that was the case. Ouch!

Once they had left the downtown area, Malika curled up atop Zarhya's saddle and paying little attention to their surroundings, the pavement vanished. But Adara was surprised to see that there were actually signposts marking the dirt lanes, to tell travelers where they led. Some of the roads even had names! Of course in Carlienne, where she'd spent most of the past two months, *all* of the streets had names – and pavement. But it was still astounding to her, to find such sophistication here in what she had expected to be the sleepy village of her childhood memories.

It was another lovely summer morning, one in a long string of them. This part of Rivermarch often got showers in the afternoon in summertime, which kept the hills green and the farmers happy. But for now, you couldn't ask for more perfect weather to be taking a ride out into the country. Adara felt joy welling up inside her, and burst uncharacteristically into song:

> *"O come with me my pretty little one,*
> *Come with me my darling,*
> *We'll tramp the road beneath the sun,*
> *And sleep until the morning…"*

She had a pleasant enough singing voice, a soft alto without any great strength or range. She seldom sang when anyone else was around, though. To her astonishment Stellan cut loose on the next verse with a beautiful, clear tenor:

> *"I'll weave spring flowers in your hair,*
> *And kiss away your sorrows,*
> *With me no troubles shall you bear,*
> *Tonight and on the morrow…"*

She turned in her saddle to look at him, eyes shining and faced wreathed in a smile, and Stellan's heart almost stopped. Whoa, get a grip! He commanded himself. Never had he let his heart completely off the leash, and this was no time to start. He grinned back at her, and launched into the chorus. She picked it up in harmony, and they rode the four miles to Underhill singing at the top of their lungs.

They rounded a bend, and saw Underhill shining before them. A broad fenced pasture full of cattle lay on their right hand, and at the end of the lane – with two gently rounded hills as a backdrop, the slopes of which were dotted with white sheep – stood the farm. The house was not really anything like the country chateau belonging to Viscount Luis de Grenvale, which edifice Adara had saved from being burned to the ground. But as farmhouses went, it was damned impressive.

The building was more than eighty feet long, two storeys high, and built of the golden local stone – not that gray granite from north of the Willough. Adara guessed it must have been put up close to a hundred years ago, from the style of the architecture and the weathered appearance of its exterior.

The house was the centerpiece of a sprawling collection of farm buildings – half a dozen large barns, something that looked like a chicken house, a smokehouse, and several other small buildings that might possibly be residences for some of the farm laborers. What a spread! A large duck pond stood off to one side, with fat gray geese cropping the grass around it.

There was even a broad portico out in front, providing shelter at the main house's front entrance, and as Adara and Stellan pulled up beneath it and made to dismount a youngish man dressed like a farm hand came up. "You must be Miss Adara and her friend," he said with a friendly grin.

The welcoming expression turned to one of alarm as Malika stood up on the saddle and stretched, then hopped down and looked around with interest. Those ducks over yonder smelled like breakfast. "Stay with me," Adara sent silently, backing up the suggestion with a hint of command. Aloud, she said "Malika, by me!" and made a hand gesture that suggested the semigryph was something like a trained hunting dog.

"I'll keep her away from the livestock," Adara promised, and the man nodded reluctantly. I want this thing off my wings, Malika sent, gazing up at Adara with her lambent yellow eyes. They were rounder than a cat's, more like an owl's – and indeed, semigryphs' hunting style was closer to that of owls. Adara put her mind into the little creature's body for a moment, keeping one hand on Zarhya's flank to steady herself. There was no pain from the broken wing, but a great deal of itching.

Soon, she promised. They got their baggage down off the horses' backs, and the ranch hand led them around to the carriage house in the rear. So grand was the entrance Adara was half expecting to be met by a butler; but it was Elana herself who came to her knock. Her face lit up with delight. "You're here!" she crowed. Then her gaze fell on Malika.

"This is the semigryph?" she asked, eyes alight with interest. She'd never seen one before, as they preferred high, rocky terrain near forests. "May I touch her?" Make nice, Adara sent, and Malika sat on her haunches.

"It's all right, you can pet her," she told her mother.

Adara's injured animal companion had been mentioned during their long get-together yesterday afternoon, but at the time she'd been happily sleeping off a meal of grain-fed rats in the hotel's stable loft. After petting the softly-furred little creature and cooing over her for a minute, Elana stood upright again. "Sorry, I didn't mean to leave you standing on the stoop with all your baggage. Come on inside."

They trooped in, and were soon shown up a flight of stairs to a pair of modest bedrooms. The accommodations were considerably more rustic than those at the Willoughby Hotel, but more homelike too. "Are you sure you're all right with Malika being in the house, Mama?" Adara asked. It didn't appear that the Underhill family had any house pets.

"She'll let you know if she needs to go outside, right?" Elana asked, and received a nod in reply. "Then, no problem. It's probably better for her to be inside with us than out there with the ducks and chickens."

"I can keep her from attacking them," Adara assured her mother. "But if she's not let out to hunt we'll need to feed her something. She'll eat almost anything but prefers raw meat."

They adjourned downstairs again, Adara, Stellan, and Malika trailing behind the lady of the house like a flock of mismatched ducklings. Elana led them to the kitchen, an enormous room with a gigantic cast iron box at one side of it and an open wood fire covered in grates sitting beneath a huge chimney.

A large, plump woman of middle years was in the midst of putting a pan of bread rolls into the box, which was evidently an oven. After closing the door she looked up and smiled broadly at the sight of her mistress and the girl who was unmistakably the long-lost Adara.

She was close to Adara's height but about three times as wide, and she marched right up and enfolded the surprised girl in a well-cushioned hug. "Oh, I would know you anywhere!" she exclaimed fondly. Elana smiled.

"Adara, this is Caraline Baker. Caraline's been cooking for Joseph's family since he was a teenager."

"Pleased to meet you, Caraline," Adara said, extending a hand. The woman seemed sweet and motherly, but she wasn't used to being embraced by complete strangers.

"And this is Malika," Elana went on, gesturing to the semigryph. Caraline looked the animal over for a moment or two.

"That's not a cat, is it?" she asked.

Malika lifted a hind leg and began scratching at the cloth. Off *now*, she sent, or I'll take it off myself! Adara bent and began undoing the knots. As soon they had come free, the cloth began to fall away and the semigryph wriggled out of her grasp and flapped her wings. Caraline gasped.

Malika's wingspan had not yet reached the nearly eight feet it would have when she was fully grown, but it was still long enough to make those around her get out of the way. She shook out her feathers, and then folded the wings along her body before sitting on her haunches again with her fluffy tail wrapped around her. She looked quite pleased with herself.

Squatting beside her little charge, Adara palpated the wing that had been broken. She could feel a hard knot of bone beneath the skin and feathers. How could such a break have healed in only a little more than a week? Take it easy with that, she sent silently, and the semigryph projected a sense of disdain. It was *her* body, and she would do what she wanted with it. Except that Adara had the ability to take over that body – something Malika knew but preferred to ignore.

"Do you have some fresh meat for Malika?" Elana asked the cook. The older woman broke from her fascination.

"Certainly," she said, turning to a large wooden cabinet that stood in another corner of the room. She opened a tightly-latched door to reveal that the cabinet appeared to be thickly insulated and lined with tin. A cold chest!

Some homes in the area around Carlienne had this modern convenience, with ice deliveries available so that householders could keep perishable foods cold. Adara stood by looking on with interest as Caraline rummaged inside and came out with a hunk of what looked like beef sirloin. With a razor-sharp kitchen knife, she quickly carved off a bowlful of little chunks and put it down on the floor for the semigryph.

I love her, Malika sent as she scrambled for the treat. After she had finished wolfing it down, she sat cleaning her fur and feathers. She showed no inclination to leave the kitchen. "I think you've just made a friend, Caraline," Adara said with a smile.

As they were sitting around the parlor again, a tall fortyish man came in through the back door, stamping his boots on the mat. His resemblance to Jaime and Leana was unmistakable. He smiled at the guests, his eyes lighting on Adara. He had not met Elana until she was in her middle twenties, but he could well imagine she'd have looked almost exactly like this girl when she was in her late teens. He warmed to her immediately, even though they had not spoken.

Elana jumped to her feet and hugged her husband, who stood four inches taller than she. Hmm, Adara thought, noting his rough garb. Joseph Underhill's role on the farm might be managerial, but it was clear he didn't mind getting "hands on" with the other farm work. He'd probably been doing chores around this place since he was old enough to walk.

"Excuse me," he told them, "I'm just going to wash up and change my clothes. It'll be time for lunch soon." He vanished for a few minutes, and returned looking considerably more like a prosperous landowner and less like someone you'd hire to muck out your stables. He favored both Adara and Stellan with warm handshakes, welcoming them to Underhill and inviting them to stay for as long as they liked.

Adara was surprised, when the midday meal was served, to find that it was shared by more than a dozen of the farm's hired hands as well as the family – all seated together around a long dining table in Underhill House's formal dining room. The children didn't join them, being away at a neighboring farm spending the day with friends. "They'll be back for supper," Elana promised. "Jaime has his own horse now, and Leana a pony. They ride all over the district by themselves."

After lunch they all – Adara, Stellan, and their hosts – mounted horses and went for a tour of the hundred acres immediately surrounding the house. Cattle and sheep were pastured all over the district, Joseph told them, but most of the farm's action was closer to home.

Dairy cattle were milked twice daily in a long milking shed, butter was churned, cheeses were made. The sheep had been sheared in early spring, the fleeces processed. Hayfields dotted the area nearer the house, awaiting harvest in another month or two. It would be stored for winter fodder, when grazing was sparse. There were hogs, chickens, geese and ducks, and quite a few sheepdogs about the place. The barns housed a goodly population of cats, living more or less wild as they kept the rodent population in check.

"That semigryph of yours looks like she'd be a good mouser," Joseph remarked as they left the barns.

"She's just a baby," Adara informed him, "but she's already begun to show some skill in that area. I'm afraid she won't stick around long, though, once she's able to fly. She *is* a wild animal, even if she seems to have bonded with me."

"I've never seen the like," her stepfather replied. He had proved to be cordial enough, clearly prepared to welcome the daughter his wife had thought lost; but they sensed a certain reserve about him. As both Adara and Stellan were a bit reserved as well, they got along fine.

No thunderstorms had materialized today, and the afternoon was downright hot. Adara pulled out a handkerchief and blotted her brow beneath the brim of the hat she was wearing, and looked out to the southeast where a small forest seemed to be winding down out of the low hills. "Is there a creek over there?" she asked, and Elana smiled.

"It supplies most of what we need for watering the stock," she acknowledged, "though we do have several wells on the property. Just around the bend of that hill on the left there's a little waterfall and a swimming hole. Joseph and his sisters used to play hooky from their chores and go skinny-dipping there, on hot summer afternoons."

Adara turned toward Stellan, and they exchanged a glance that spoke volumes. "That sounds wonderful," Adara remarked casually. "I think we might want to go over there after we finish the tour."

"That was about it," Joseph said. "I wish I could join you, but I've got work to do."

"Me too," Elana said. "The kids and I will be going into town tomorrow to sell at the market stand, and I need to get ready for that. You'll be back to join us for supper?"

"Oh, yes," Adara said, with a secret smile.

Chapter 10

Zarhya and Zoli snorted as they came in under the trees. The little forest was only an oak woodland less than a mile across, the trees following the course of the narrow stream as it wound down out of the hills for miles. Yet within their spotty shade, it was degrees cooler than it had been down in the farmyard.

Adara and Stellan spoke little as the horses followed the narrow trail that ran along the creek's western bank, Zarhya in the lead. In the heat of the summer afternoon, there was little sound but the tinkling of the water, flowing over the stones of its bed; and the gentle clomping of the horses' hooves as they picked their way along. The buzzing of insects was a background note, almost unnoticed.

Around half a mile upstream from where they'd entered the woods, they heard a much louder splashing and the tree canopy opened out a little. Ahead, a waterfall six feet tall and less than ten feet wide poured down from a cleft between two rocks to feed a crystalline pool no more than twenty feet from side to side and somewhat longer. Boulders lined it on the east, but here on the west bank the pool's waters lapped a narrow sandy beach. Perfect!

They dismounted and unsaddled the horses, swapping bridles for halters. After taking a drink at the water's edge, Zarhya and Zoli wandered a few paces away to crop the grass growing in the strip of sunlight that ran along this side of the pool.

Adara, who'd put on a lightweight cotton shirt with her leather traveling pants for this afternoon's outing, was sweating profusely. She bent to scoop up some of the pool's water in her hands, and splash it across her face. "Ooh, it's cooler than I expected!" she exclaimed. This was no glacier-fed mountain stream, icy enough to turn you blue in a minute – like the Willough had been last spring, when she'd attempted to take a bath at dawn. But it was definitely cold enough to be refreshing.

Rose crept up Adara's neck as she thought of that bath, more than three months ago now. At the time she'd been outraged that Ferdyn had followed her, freezing her ass off and embarrassed as hell to be caught in the nude by that importunate young man and his

58

obvious desire to get into her pants. Thinking about it now, she realized just how much that desire had beckoned to her. She glanced sidewise at Stellan and saw him standing motionless, devouring her with his gaze. She felt no outrage, now.

Still, Adara found herself suddenly feeling awkward. She hadn't had enough experience with this sort of thing to be all cool and casual about it. Do I just strip off and hop into the water, she wondered? Or should I let Stellan undress me with something besides his eyes?

The fact that she was hot, sweaty, and a little dusty decided it for Adara. Declaring "Whew!" she sat down on a nearby boulder and kicked off her boots, removing her stockings and wiggling her toes in the damp sand with a sigh of contentment. Then she unlaced her shirt and pulled it off over her head. Stellan continued gazing at her, his dark eyes boring into her soul, seemingly lost in the moment.

Adara carried her boots a little away from the beach and hung her shirt on a convenient tree branch, then wriggled out of the leather pants and her drawers, and hung them up as well. She turned back to find Stellan looking at her now with an expression of helpless longing, tight black pants strained across the crotch. Mmm!

"Last one in's a troll," she caroled with a mischievous grin, and dashed past him to splash into the water. The bottom fell off sharply and Adara could see that it was more than ten feet deep in the middle; so she did a shallow dive. Oh, the water felt marvelous!

On the bank, Stellan was doing an impression of a man who's just discovered that his clothing has been invaded by a colony of stinger ants. A slow grin had appeared on his face. He had grown up along the banks of the Grandeon a few hundred miles from its sources in the Crestans – not an ideal stretch of water in which to learn how to swim. But he had picked up the skill, like so many others, in his travels over the past five years. He could swim well enough not to drown, at least.

In less than a minute Stellan had rid himself of boots, stockings, pants, drawers, and vest and dived in after Adara – his cock standing straight up. She caught a quick glimpse of it before he dived, surprised to note that while he was a much smaller man overall than

was Ferdyn, there was not that much difference in the size of their…
equipment.

He swam down to the bottom and then rose to the surface,
gasping. "It's a *lot* cooler than *I* expected!" he exclaimed. His
erection was already ebbing. Adara grinned at him, her dark hair
plastered to her head as she treaded water in the center of the pool.
"Just wait a few seconds, you'll get used to it!" she replied
cheerfully, then added "Troll…"

"A troll, am I?" Stellan demanded with a mock snarl. "I'll get
you…" he lunged for her, but Adara easily evaded his grasp. Diving,
she swam underwater in the direction of the waterfall. The water was
considerably colder at this end of the pool. She came up sputtering,
and he spotted her immediately. Grinning and sticking out her
tongue, she dived once more.

Stellan chased Adara around the swimming hole in growing
frustration for another minute or so. Then she seemed to have
vanished. The water was clear, and there was no sign of her on the
bottom. He glanced up. Aha… Suddenly Adara, standing on a
slippery boulder behind the falls, found herself seized in an iron
grasp.

"Arr, a fair maiden!" Stellan growled. "We trolls *like* fair
maidens! We like to eat them up!" Without releasing his grip, he
bent and ran his mouth along her neck, nibbling and sucking. As
Adara made no attempt to get away, instead gasping in pleasure, he
pulled away from her enough to take one of her stiff nipples in his
mouth. She moaned.

Adara ran her fingers over Stellan's firmly muscled abdomen,
then reached lower. Despite the cold, his cock was hard again. As
she squeezed, it was his turn to moan. Releasing her nipple from his
mouth, he pressed his body to hers and murmured in her ear.
"Adara…" – gasp – "I'm freezing! Can we go back out to where the
water is warmer please?" She smiled into his shoulder and gave his
cock another tug. Then she dived again, swimming under the falls
and back toward the middle of the pool.

In moments they were half lying, half floating on the sandy
bottom on the side of the pool that was in full sun, color returning to
their white bodies. Stellan took Adara in his arms and kissed her, as

his right hand slipped down her body and between her legs. He inserted two fingers between her nether lips, pressing against her clit, and she nearly came on the spot. Oh, it had been too long!

Kissing her fervently, panting, Stellan looked into Adara's eyes. "Yes?" he asked, "Yes?"

"Yes, Stellan, yes!" she moaned, almost a plea. He guided his rigid member inside her. "Maridem, yes!" she squealed, thrusting her pelvis forward to receive him as he pushed inside. All the way in, filling her up, hot and hard and wonderful.

There was frenzied thrashing in the water, the horses grazing placidly nearby giving it scarcely a glance, and in all too short a time it was over. "Been a long time for you, too?" Adara murmured softly, gazing up into Stellan's night-dark eyes. He kissed her again, long and hard.

"I'm not through with you, not by a long sight," he growled. He glanced toward the shore. "Did you by any chance bring a blanket?"

Chapter 11

Stellan and Adara returned from their visit to the creek, as the sun was falling toward the western horizon, looking extremely clean, extremely pink, and extremely refreshed. She had only introduced him to the surprising pack of relatives who'd cropped up as her "friend, who's helping me with an expedition I'm going on"; but if any of the adults had any doubts about the nature of that friendship, there could be no doubts at the dinner table that night.

As they shared the evening meal with every person at Underhill except the kitchen staff, who habitually took their meals in the kitchen, the way they sat close together, the glances they stole from downcast eyes, told everyone with eyes to see that the two were lovers. Elana wondered it at it, but tried not to pass judgment. Adara was an adult, on her own now, and clearly a young woman in command of her own life. And Stellan, once she had gotten to know him a little, seemed like a nice enough young man.

After a simple but delicious dinner of roast beef, roasted potatoes, fresh bread rolls, steamed greens, and fresh melon for dessert, the hands went on the way to their own quarters while the family gathered in the parlor. "Elana mentioned you are off soon on some kind of quest?" Joseph asked after they were seated, getting the conversation started.

"Nothing so dangerous as a quest," Adara assured them. Certainly unknown dangers might await them in the mountains to the north, but she wanted to downplay both the possible harm to herself and the reasons why she wasn't the slightest bit afraid. Even after their hours of passionate lovemaking on the banks of the stream this afternoon, she wanted to keep a few things hidden from Stellan until she got to know him better. He was a wonderful lover, that was for certain; but was he a truly reliable companion? Time would tell.

Adara had brought one of her books down from her bedroom, and she opened it to the page in question – the one that had decided her to make this particular ancient mystery her project. Accompanying the text on that page was an etching of a squat, muscular figure that looked roughly human. More human than the Swinzen, certainly.

"Do you all know what kobolds are?" Adara asked.

It was Joseph who replied, "Aren't they mythical beings similar to trolls, but said to live deep in the bowels of the earth and mine gems and ores?" he asked. It was common knowledge, and widely accepted.

Adara smiled at him slyly. "Most people today believe the kobolds were only a myth," she admitted, "but they're wrong. While I was in Carlienne I enlisted the Royal Magus' help in identifying some subjects that I might delve into now that I'm free to go exploring. Up until a few hundred years ago, everyone in the areas around the mountains knew the kobolds, because they came up out of their burrows regularly to trade with the humans and other elves who lived above."

Her audience was confounded. "*Other* elves?" Elana asked, and her daughter nodded.

"Cruztan – that's the Royal Magus, a very nice old man even if he *could* turn you into a cockroach with a wave of his fingers – believes that kobolds are just another race of elf. He thinks all of the long-lived human-shaped sentients on Eorla share a common ancestry, but that at some unimaginably distant time in the past there was a cataclysm, or maybe some magical event, that split them into the races we know today."

The elves of the island kingdom of Elyrion, whose incursion into the coastal area of Tanar known as Elvany twenty years before had triggered the kingdom's last major war, were a tall and willowy folk known as Sea Elves or merudur. They were the elves most familiar to the humans of Tanar, but there were many other sorts scattered around the continent – and still more, here and there, on the planet Q'ur's many other land masses.

Nobody knew what to say to Adara's suggestion. The Forest Elves of Nordstan were seldom seen in this part of the world, and the Green Elves who inhabited the jungles of northern Frigan, the continent immediately to Eorla's south, were seldom seen even by their closest neighbors. They waited for her to continue, and she did.

"Whether the kobolds were truly a kind of elf we'll probably never know," she said. "No one has seen a kobold for hundreds of years. At the places where they met to trade with men, from one year to next they just vanished. And none they traded with, it turned out, actually knew just where the kobolds lived. There was no way to go check on them, find out what happened."

"They traded a lot before then?" Joseph asked. As a man of business, trade was a major concern for him. "They had many ores dug from beneath the earth, many gems, and much skill in working them," Adara said. She found herself now in the position Ferdyn had been in a few months ago, delivering lectures. Damn, she sure missed him for his fund of knowledge, if for no other reason.

"But as you can imagine, not much food grows beneath the earth," Adara went on. "Men wanted the beautiful jewelry and fine weapons the kobolds produced, and the kobolds were eager for the enrichment in their diet made possible by trading with men. They traded for items like turnips, cabbage, woven cloth, leather goods — all the things they could not produce themselves. No one could imagine they would simply stop showing up to trade without mentioning there was a problem, so it was assumed that something catastrophic had happened to them – a plague, perhaps, or a massive cave-in."

"But surely, a cave-in would only affect one… tribe, or whatever they had?" Elana asked.

"Not necessarily," Adara explained. "For all any of their human trading partners knew, the various trading missions who met with them at the enclaves scattered around northern Tanar and southern Nordstan had all come from the same underground city. Elves are always less numerous than humans, and the kobolds even more so, or so it would seem. There were probably no more than a couple of hundred of them seen above ground at any one time. They usually came to the trading enclaves but once a year, near harvest time."

Malika had joined them after supper, and was now curled up beside Adara on the settee, purring as her friend ran her fingers over the semigryph's soft fur. Her feathers were as soft, each one covered in a fine noise-dampening fuzz like the feathers of an owl. Jaime was on the other side, also petting the little creature, with Leana beside him. Both kids had been astounded and delighted to arrive home from their friends' house and see the fabled semigryph curled up on a pile of flour sacks in Caraline's kitchen.

"So you're saying it's possible kobolds were as rare as your little friend there," Joseph said, gesturing toward Malika.

"Who can say?" Adara replied. "Certainly they were human in a way, living in societies – something semigryphs do not. And from their skill in making jewelry in weapons, they must have had some significant numbers engaged in mining, smelting, smithing, and metalwork. But whatever the case, from that first year when the kobolds failed to arrive for the annual trade gathering no man has claimed to have seen one."

"So is that what you're going to do, Adara?" Jaime asked eagerly. "Go find the lost kobolds?" She smiled wryly at him.

"Not exactly," she replied. "I think after seven hundred years they're not just lost, they're gone. But in my researches I discovered a mention of a trader, a thousand years back, who befriended one of the kobolds who came regularly to the trading enclave that once existed near Feingeld, in Northmarch. He wrote in his journal that his friend told him of a site less than forty miles from there, accessed through a tunnel into a mountain known as the Dunblitz."

"A place where the kobolds lived, then?" Jaime asked. Adara shook her head.

"A place where they died, or rather where they were laid to rest," she said. "The ancient trader reported that his friend had told him the kobolds had had one great king, a ruler over all their people, who had died after a reign of a thousand years. So beloved was he that the kobolds had carved him a tomb high up within the Dunblitz, the Thunder Cloud as they called it."

Everyone was gazing at Adara raptly now, Stellan more than any of them. This was the most information he had yet gotten out of her regarding the quest he was to help her on. "The tomb was still a long way below the rocks of the mountain, of course," she went on, "but the people this king had ruled over lived far deeper than that. They were enshrining him, with all of his possessions and the archives of his reign, in a place where he could be above them forever more."

Stellan's dark eyes glittered at the word "possessions," easily conjuring a mental image of what possessions a king might have, who ruled over a people famed for their skill in making weapons and jewelry. His heart beat a little faster – though not nearly as fast as it had, earlier today.

Jaime's eyes, too, were wide with excitement. "Do you have a treasure map, Adara?" She smiled indulgently at him, her little sort-of brother.

"A map would be nice," she admitted. "What I do have is a pretty explicit description of the landmarks that should lead me to where the air shaft is located. Assuming that nothing has changed very much since a thousand years ago. Now if it turns out the kobolds were wiped out by a cave-in, this Tomb of the Kobold King might be buried under a mountain of rubble. But I have to go see for myself, and Stellan is going to help me."

Chapter 12

Stellan stole into Adara's bedroom, next door to his own, not long after the household had gone to bed. The bed proved to be a great deal more comfortable than the thin picnic blanket on the strand had been. As they lay in the afterglow, with her snuggled into his side naked atop the coverlet, his hand fell on the Darkshield. Earlier today, he'd assumed she had not wanted to remove her jewelry lest it be lost amid the leaf litter surrounding the pool.

"You still have your necklace on," he said sleepily. Finally, after making love to Adara for the fifth time today, he was beginning to feel sated. Or at least, tired enough to rest for a few hours before going at it again. She was not what he thought of as his "type" – his liaisons in the past had often been with small, cuddly women. But there was something about Adara that he found unbelievably sexy. He wanted her again and again. That he might be falling in love with her, was a thought he'd dismissed as absurd.

"I never take it off," she murmured in his ear, stroking his chest. "My mother gave it to me when I was five, and for years it was the only thing I had of her. But now it's like a part of me. And it's waterproof, so why not wear it?" He grunted noncommittally, and kissed her forehead.

"As jewelry goes, it's a little… dark. Looks like something *I'd* wear…"

"Hey, just because I don't go around dressed in black all the time, doesn't mean I'm not a woman of mystery with dark, sorcerous powers…" She ran a fingernail down his chest, and tweaked the nipple. He shuddered slightly, and rolled over to face her, drawing her tight to him. He kissed her deeply, then growled, "I am fully aware of your sorcerous powers. Look what you did to me." His cock had gone hard again.

The following day Stellan and Adara rode into town alongside Elana driving the wagon, with Jaime and Leana sitting beside her on the bench. The bed of the wagon was loaded with goods that they'd sell, either at their stand in the market square or to be offered at Willoughby Mercantile. The tight bond forged between the

Willoughbys and their widowed sister-in-law when they had taken her in after the demon attack would never be broken.

At the breakfast table Adara and Stellan had sat side by side, devouring biscuits and gravy with scrambled eggs and discussing the outfitting of what they were starting to call their "Kobold Expedition." She was very pleased to learn that he had some experience with both mountaineering and spelunking, and had some excellent suggestions about what they should bring along.

So, the plan was for Adara to hang out with her mother and younger siblings, helping to man the market stand, while Stellan went out with their list and a large purse of gold to obtain the items they were going to need. As she handed over the money Adara had a momentary flash of it, and Stellan, vanishing out of her life forever. But that was ludicrous. They were beginning to break down each other's walls, and she thought she knew him better than that. If he planned to run out on her, it wouldn't be until their big score was in hand.

There had been no passionate declarations of love like she'd had from Ferdyn, and Adara was all right with that. Stellan was gorgeous, mysterious, intriguing, and good company. She could just enjoy having him as a friend and companion, a hot lover between her legs to light up her nights. It didn't have to be another big romance. She'd already had her heart broken once this year, and that was enough.

Today was a regular market day, and business at the Underhill Farm stand was brisk. Many local farmers had brought produce and sold it right out of their wagons parked helter-skelter in the square itself, making the scene chaotic but entertaining.

They didn't even bother closing up for lunch, just buying some apricots and cherries from one of the other vendors to eat with the bread, cheese, cold sliced ham, pickles, and ale they'd brought from home. In between sales and digging out merchandise, Adara had plenty of time to talk with her mother and with the kids as well.

Stellan returned several times during the day, bringing list items he'd purchased in town to store in the wagon before making another foray. Toward two in the afternoon he sauntered up to the stand, munching on fried potato strips in a paper packet glistening with oil.

"Mmph, these are good," he said enthusiastically. "You want some?" He offered the packet, and both kids took a few but Adara and her mother politely declined. They didn't want to get grease all over the merchandise.

"Where'd you get that?" Adara asked, looking around. She hadn't noticed any street vendors offering hot cooked food.

"From the old inn down by the waterfront," Stellan replied with a gesture. "Their fare is pretty basic, but what they have is good. I've usually stayed there whenever I'm in Willoughby."

The kids had extended their awe of big sister Adara to her friend Stellan, as well. He was young and dashing, and clearly a bold adventurer just like she was since she was bringing him along on her expedition to find a legendary tomb. They were hanging on his words as he told Adara, "I talked to a trader from up Behrenstein way. Did you say we had to go to Feingeld in order to follow the directions to the Dunblitz?"

"That's right," Adara confirmed. "The ancient trader was given instructions based on traveling from there, since that was where he met with his kobold friend. I guess the place used to be a big deal but with no kobolds and the gold there long since gone, I suppose it's little more than a ghost town now."

"That's what my trader said," Stellan confirmed – stuffing the last of the potato strips into his mouth and then pulling out a handkerchief to wipe his fingers. He was fairly fastidious, for a man of his time who so often lived out of doors. "But he told me the main road between Willoughby and Behrenstein goes right past the mountain cutoff up to Feingeld. Just since the bridge has gone up, the Duke of Northmarch has paved the entire stretch from the bridge north and west, and up into the pass, trying to make it passable for more of the year. The road to Feingeld's not paved, of course, but the trader said it's pretty hard to miss. It's the only thing bigger than a goat track leading up into the Ratskells off the main road."

"Excellent!" Adara said, beaming. Not only was Stellan good in bed, he was demonstrating some very useful qualities as a questing companion. Might they become a long-term team, a legendary duo? Oh, get a grip, she told herself. Just because her body wanted her to fall head-over-heels in love with this man who stirred her to her soul, didn't mean her mind was going along with the program. "Did he say how far up from the main road to Feingeld?"

Stellan nodded. "Around fifty miles," he said. "They built the main road through the foothills, so that winter snows are less of a problem. It takes a sharp right turn and goes up over the Foendahl pass to Behrenstein north of the mountains. But it could take us a couple of days to cross that fifty miles on a road that hasn't been improved in several centuries." Adara nodded. "We'd better bring along extra food for us and grain for the horses," she said.

Elana had freed herself from her most recent customer and was listening to the tail end of their exchange. She put an arm around her daughter and squeezed. "Don't you worry about any of that, dear," she said warmly. "Caraline will pack you enough trail meals for a week on the road, more if you want. And we've got enough grain stacked up at the farm to bury the house in."

Adara would have preferred to pay – she had enough money, essentially, to buy anything she could imagine wanting to own. But she sensed her mother wanted to… be motherly, in essence. To provide her wayward chick with something, after missing out on most of her childhood. So she squeezed her back and said only, "Thanks, Mama…"

That evening they were all once again sitting around the parlor, talking after dinner. Adara had only had the one adventure as yet, and they'd already discussed that at length. She was sure Stellan had had dozens of them – after all, he'd admitted to leaving home at the age of sixteen. And he was now twenty-one. Much closer to her own age than Ferdyn was. Adara wondered idly if Stellan's relative youth accounted for his astonishing sexual energy. But as for recounting his adventures, he seemed reluctant to discuss them in any detail.

"So," Joseph said, "You've got everything you need for your expedition?" Adara and Stellan both nodded.

"Thanks so much for all the provisions," he said.

"You're leaving in the morning, then?"

"We'll be back afterward to tell you all how it went," Adara promised. "It'll probably take us no more than a couple of weeks there and back…"

"Unless we have to hire pack mules in Behrenstein to haul out all the treasure," Stellan put in, with a grin. Adara elbowed him in the ribs.

He held up his hands, as if to surrender. "What," he protested, "it's not as if the kobolds are going to object. We can be respectful to king whatsisname's corpse, you can gather all your archaeological data from his archives – though I wonder where you're going to find somebody who can read kobold scrolls – and we'll carry off any spare gems and weapons that are lying around. The king's not going to miss them…"

Adara sighed. Of course, it was the lack of this attitude in Ferdyn that had led to their parting, so perhaps she couldn't object. And even though it was true that she expected to have no need of additional money for the rest of what should, with luck, be the many years remaining in her life, the idea of treasure still excited her a bit too.

"I want to go with you!" Jaime crowed, eyes sparkling with excitement. "It'll be so amazing, and educational too!" he added, for the benefit of his mother.

"Out of the question," Joseph said.

"But Papa, Adara said it's not going to be dangerous! I've got plenty of warm winter clothes, and Figi is a strong horse. I could bring my bow and help hunt for game, and with Adara and Stellan armed to the teeth, what could go wrong? *Please* say I can go!"

Elana and her husband exchanged glances. "What could go wrong," she said sweetly to her son. "Let's see…" she began ticking off threats on her fingers, "avalanches, rockslides, brown bears, dragons, gryphons…" Running out of fingers, she switched to the other hand and continued. "Rocs, bandits, poisonous snakes, snow lions, wolf packs…" Jaime's open, friendly face had taken on a very pained expression. He glared sullenly up at his mother, and she just gave him a look of martyred patience.

"You're letting Adara go," he mumbled, knowing how stupid that sounded.

"Adara is an *adult*," Elana pronounced. "I'm not 'letting' her do anything, she can do whatever she wants. In five years, if Adara is willing to take you along on her adventures, go right ahead. But not when you're twelve years old. Do you understand?" Lower lip thrust out, looking close to tears from the embarrassment of being put in his place in front of the new big sister he'd come to idolize, Jaime merely nodded.

Adara patted him on the shoulder. "Sorry, Jaime," she said. "But Mom's right. Just because we don't have to fight our way past an army of demons or defeat a powerful sorcerer doesn't mean our expedition isn't dangerous for someone who doesn't have the skills and experience we have. Five years will go by fast. Practice your woodcraft and your archery, and when you're old enough I promise I'll take you along. All right?"

Chapter 13

They didn't get off to as early a start as they'd hoped. For one thing, expecting that this was their last chance to have sex in a comfortable, warm bed for the immediate future, they'd stayed up a bit later than planned. Then of course there had been a huge family breakfast, hugs and kisses all around (at least between Adara and her new family; Stellan settled for handshakes), and the question of whether Malika was going to come along.

Though Caraline lacked Adara's ability to speak with her mind to mind, the cook and the juvenile semigryph had bonded during their short stay at Underhill. She seemed quite content to spend her days in the kitchen napping or feasting on freshly chopped meat, and her nights making sure that no mice invaded the space.

Yet Adara feared that Malika's contentment with taking on the role of a housecat would not last – and semigryphs were not intended to be pets. Best case she would fly away, worst she would have to be put down for attacking the livestock. So it was a relief for Adara when she sent "Coming, now?" and the small creature padded to her side. She meowed politely to Caraline, then followed Adara out the door.

The entire family, and several of the farm employees who had come to feel close to the visitors, gathered in front of the house to see them off. Malika was perched on the front of Zarhya's saddle, and not only Sadiq but both riding horses were loaded down with packs of supplies. Jaime seemed to have recovered from his pique, and stood with his parents and little sister waving cheerfully as Adara and Stellan turned and began the short journey back to town.

Stellan heaved a sigh as they got under way. His feelings were in turmoil – an undercurrent of lust directed at Adara, excitement at the prospects for a big score in the kobold king's tomb, and a contradictory mix of sadness in parting from the people who had welcomed him so kindly into their midst, and relief that he and Adara would now be alone. There was more than one reason why he'd taken up the life of a solitary wanderer, and he found himself uncomfortable in situations where he was expected to be sociable for days at a time.

They trotted across the broad Willoughby Bridge at midmorning, and soon found themselves in terrain much different from that to the south. This bank of the river was much steeper and rockier, though the Ratskells were still nearly a hundred miles away to the north. Though that range was far lower than the Crestans, three hundred miles to the east, there were a few peaks that still had snow on them even now in Dayrule, clearly visible through the haze.

As Stellan's Northmarch trader had reported, the road they traveled was broad and paved with stone. The duchy of Northmarch might lack for good level agricultural land and long growing seasons, but it was rich in granite, minerals, and timber. They made good time through the day, stopping only briefly in early afternoon for a picnic lunch of sandwiches and fruit packed by Caraline. Early evening found them well north and west of Willoughby, and they took the horses down off the road into a mixed forest of oaks and pines to look for a place to camp for the night.

Adara watched with pleasure as Stellan immediately set about unloading the horses, rubbing them down, and providing them with grain to eat. They'd managed to camp beside a small stream, so water was not a problem. Shaking herself out of her reverie, she turned to setting up their tent and scraping out a fire pit. Malika had gone off into the woods, exploring, as soon as it became clear they intended to stop.

Caraline had provided them many bars of trail bread – a mixture of dried meat, suet, honey, nuts, and dried fruits – which required no cooking and was dense in nutrition. But as long as they had a comfortable campsite and a fire, Adara decided she might as well cook something. Stellan didn't notice how suddenly the campfire flared to life, busy as he was with the animals. By the time he joined her, a cooking pot was set above the flames and she was cutting chunks of ham for a bean soup.

Stellan astounded Adara by producing a small cithara from his pack. Stirring the pot, she asked him curiously, "Did you forget to tell me you're also a bard?" He smiled into her eyes. They might still be keeping secrets from one another, but in becoming lovers they had opened the door to intimacy.

"I'm not actually a bard," he said, sitting on one of the sturdy folding stools they'd brought and beginning to tune his instrument. "I've loved to play and sing since I was around Jaime's age, but it's only for my own enjoyment – or the enjoyment of my friends."

"You have many of those?" Adara asked, seeing an opening. When she had been traveling with Ferdyn it seemed she was running into his old pals around every corner, making her feel like an outsider. But in her time with Stellan so far, it had been he who was the stranger.

"Not too many," he replied with the faintest hint of sadness. "The road called to me, and I took it. And it's hard to have close friends when you're on the move all the time." Adara reached across to squeeze his hand.

"You have me," she said softly. The look in his eyes took her aback with its intensity; but almost as quickly as it appeared, it was gone.

Smiling wryly, Stellan brought his fingers down across the cithara's strings and produced a rich chord. Then he went into a delicate, tinkling melody before singing:

> *The wind doth blow today, my love,*
> *And comes down drops of rain,*
> *I ne'er had me but one true love,*
> *In cold grave she was lain..."*

The ballad was a mournful one, and ran on for quite a few verses. The lover vows to watch at his true love's grave, then begs a kiss from her cold lips. Eventually he dies beside her. Adara wore a slight smile of bemusement. "Pretty music," she said, "but awfully dark. Do you know any happier tunes?"

Mischief glittered in Stellan's dark eyes as he struck up another melody:

> *The fourteenth day of Flora, of all days of*
> *the year,*
> *A lovely lady, fresh and gay, did privately*
> *appear.*
> *Hard by a riverside got she, and did sing*
> *loud, the rather,*

75

*For she was sure she was secure, and had
intent to bath her*

Adara burst into a brilliant smile. The rogue! He continued:

*With glittering glancing jealous eyes, she
shyly looks about,
To see if any lurking spies were hid to find
her out.
And being well resolved that none could
see her nakedness,
She pulled her robes off, one by one, and
did herself undress.*

The bawdy ballad might have been written by someone taking notes down at the creekside a couple of days ago! Adara found herself convulsed with laughter, even as a warm sensation rose in her loins at the memory of that afternoon. As the last notes of the song died away she got to her feet and gave the pot one more stir. Then she gently removed the cithara from Stellan's hands and set it carefully aside, before climbing into his lap.

Some hours later, as they sat beside the fire after eating, Adara mused "I hadn't expected to have to camp out, this close to a fine road." They'd passed quite a few traders' wagons moving in both directions during their ride today. "You'd think somebody would be building inns to serve all the traffic."

"I'm sure someone's working on that as we speak," Stellan replied thoughtfully. "Remember, it's only been a few years since the bridge went in and the road was paved. Come back here in another couple of years, and there'll probably be an inn on this very spot." He put his arm around her and leaned over to nibble her earlobe.

Clouds ringed the sky as they climbed higher in the foothills, and they often found themselves getting rained on. Fortunately they both had oilskin cloaks to put on over their traveling clothes, keeping them and their belongings, tied behind the saddles, dry. Sadiq's load mostly consisted of their food and fodder stores, and the equipment they'd brought for the expected descent into the mountainside.

It was after midday on their third day of travel when Adara and Stellan came upon the "road" to Feingeld. It had rained most of the previous afternoon and evening, and they had eaten trail bread for supper and again this morning for breakfast. But now the sun had come out, praise Maridem, and they were both grinning as they turned their horses to the north.

It was certainly more than a game trail or goat track, but to call the four-foot-wide, muddy and rutted trace that wound its way up switchbacks into the mountains a "road" was overstating the case. Certainly, if wheeled conveyances had once traveled here that time was long in the past.

The horses had to pick their way carefully up slippery, boulder-strewn slopes, and their progress was slowed to a crawl. But the sun was shining overhead, and both Stellan and Adara were feeling a pleasant excitement as their goal approached. Soon, tomorrow maybe, they would reach what was left of the once-thriving trade center (and mining town) of Feingeld, and begin unraveling the clues that would lead them to untold treasure – or at least, exciting discoveries.

Adara had half expected Malika to abandon them as they climbed higher. The young semigryph had become increasingly adept at ground hunting, little hampered it seemed by her wings. She had begun using them more, flapping to build up strength and even using them to encircle prey; but she didn't seem ready to try flying yet. That was what had gotten her in trouble in the first place. She accepted tidbits of dried meat from Adara, but seemed to be providing all of her own meals from the surrounding wilderness. Yet, she remained in communication with Adara and always returned.

As darkness fell that night, they broke out the winter clothes they'd brought for the first time. Malika had feasted on a fat marmot earlier, and was now curled up sleeping before the fire. Instead of their folding stools, Adara and Stellan were seated on a large, nearly-soft fallen log the campsite had provided – warming themselves and gazing into the flames without saying much.

Adara was still wrestling with the desire to lose her heart to Stellan. He had proven to be a skilled and useful companion, and had not betrayed her or proven false in any way. Why could she not be frank with him, tell him everything she had so freely admitted to Ferdyn? Was it fear of the pain that would follow should she lose him, too?

He had his arm around her, and the two of them were huddled together beneath a single voluminous wool cloak. Thank Baldor we're not here in the winter, Adara thought. She turned from the flames to find Stellan gazing at her, an expression of longing on his face, and she decided to be brave and take the first step. Squeezing his thigh and planting a sweet, gentle kiss on his lips, she said softly, "Stellan, there are some things I've been wanting to tell you, things about me you probably should know. But you've told me so little about yourself. Do you think you could... open up to me, a little? I promise I won't judge you..."

His response was to hold her more tightly and give her a deep, lingering kiss. Then he turned to stare into the fire once more. He sighed, then said "Very well. First off, what I told you about my being born in Riparre and having a lot of relatives is true."

"Mm-hm?" Adara responded, urging him to say more.

"But my family name is not Archer. That's a name I took for myself, when I fancied myself an expert bowman." Adara had seen him shoot, and he was pretty good at it – if not as good as she was, with her magically-enhanced ability to learn. She waited, and he continued – dredging the words up as if it was painful to speak them. "The rest of my family – my brothers and sisters, parents, and so forth – all proudly bear the surname du Rive."

Adara gasped involuntarily. "Du Rive? The duke's family?" Stellan nodded, his mouth twisted in a wry grin. "Old Zoltan is my father's second cousin," he said. "But Father's a third son, and our branch of the family is pretty low down in the pecking order. They're still well off, I suppose, by the standards of the common folk – probably about as wealthy and prosperous as your mother and stepfather, more or less."

"Beats living in a hovel and hoeing turnips for a living, I suppose," Adara remarked casually. It was odd, how one's standards always seemed to rise so one was never satisfied with one's lot. At least *her* standards hadn't yet caught up with her new-found fortune. "So, why did your father tell you never to darken his door again?"

Stellan turned to look into her eyes again. He looked worried. "I'm going to be completely honest with you, Adara," he said after a few moments' hesitation. "I feel more comfortable with you than I have with anyone in a long time, and it means a lot to me that you trust me."

She leaned in and kissed him again, but inside her stomach was churning. Was he about to reveal some truly awful crime? "When I was sixteen," he began, "I was a rebel. Dissatisfied with my lot in life, chafing under my father's rules, scorning society's conventions. I didn't want to live the same life my brothers did, complacent members of the minor aristocracy, going about their boring round of parties and politics. But if I was going to have the life of adventure I wanted, I was going to need some money to get started with."

"You couldn't just ask your father, or maybe your cousin the duke, to give you some I suppose?" Adara asked, though the answer seemed clear. What member of the nobility would happily finance his youngest son's ambitions to become a footloose vagabond?" Stellan barked a short laugh.

"Truth to tell," he admitted, "it did not occur to me to ask. There was some talk of buying me a commission in the military, or I might perhaps have considered going into the priesthood. I kept my own plans to myself."

"And what were those plans?" Adara asked, feeling she was finally on the verge of an important discovery.

"I seduced my cousin Rosalie, the duke's daughter. She's not quite a year younger than me, so in a way we were just two young kids exploring the ways of love together. We were both virgins. But I had ulterior motives. I used her to get me a key to the duke's treasure house. And then I made off with around six thousand marks in gold and gems."

Adara stared at him, agog. Quite an ambitious heist for a sixteen-year-old. But how the hell had he imagined he would not get caught? Stellan eyed her ruefully. "I know, it was a completely idiotic plan. And cruel to Rosie, who was a sweet kid. I'd told her we would run away together, and then I went without her – leaving her to face the music."

"That *is* pretty horrible," Adara said weakly. "So of course Rosie ratted you out when she realized she'd been had?" Stellan sighed.

"That's the most horrible part," he said. "She stayed firm. Fortunately she'd had access to those herbs you take every morning, so no child came of our union. And she never said a word about me to anyone."

"Then how did the duke know it was you who robbed him?" Adara asked.

"He didn't," came the reply. "Not really. But there was a lot of circumstantial evidence, not the least of which was that I'd vanished from Riparre without a trace. No one was ever brought up on charges, and Cousin Zoltan hushed up the whole affair. But when I sneaked back home in disguise three years later for Rosie's wedding, I spoke with Father. He'd never had any doubt that it was I who had robbed the treasury, though luckily no one had realized Rosie had had a part in it. She knows and I know, and now you know, Adara. I've never told another living soul."

A feeling of warmth suffused Adara. She felt confident that she had just heard the worst Stellan had to tell – and it wasn't so bad as all that. Hell, she could pay back the amount Stellan had taken from the duke's treasury with pocket change if she wanted to, and all of *her* wealth had technically been stolen from the Swinzen. She took Stellan in her arms and kissed him hard, murmuring "Thank you."

When they broke from the clinch Stellan's features were a mask of relief. He had half expected her to shove him backwards off the log and announce he was fired, and then she had kissed him! "So, what about you?" he asked. "Do you too harbor dark secrets, my sorceress?"

Adara smiled slyly at him. "O, many and more, my prince of thieves," she said. She called Ariel, and suddenly the flames from their fire shot skyward. Of the four, that had seemed the safest demonstration. His eyes got wide, and he looked at her questioningly. "I have... what you might call a 'friendly relationship' with the elemental spirits," she explained. "More often than not, they are happy to grant my requests. Did you not notice how quickly our campfire was lit, three days ago?"

"Oh," Stellan said softly. "Now that you mention it..."

"I have the making of many herbal potions with surprising properties," Adara went on, "though that's not so dark and mysterious I suppose. I can ride the minds of non-sentient creatures, even controlling them from a distance, and communicate with some like Malika who are more intelligent."

At this the semigryph, sleeping on the far side of the fire, opened her eyes and looked at them. Then she curled into a tighter ball and went back to sleep.

"I had wondered how it was possible you had so quickly bonded a wild animal to you," Stellan responded. "Can you do that with anything?"

"Malika's the only creature I've sent my mind to who's been able to talk back, not that it's exactly words she's using," Adara admitted. "And I've never tried riding two different creatures at the same time. But I suppose that might be possible."

Stellan drew her to him and kissed her tenderly on the lips. "I'm guessing your black necklace is not just a keepsake?" he asked quietly. She gave him a questioning look. Was she so transparent?

"It's an ancient magical artifact," she said flatly. "It's been passed down through the female line of my family for many generations, though supposedly it once belonged to a completely different family over on the east side of the Crestans."

"And it makes you irresistible to men, right?" Stellan asked, only half joking as he squeezed her tight. Boy, even with the roaring fire it was getting cold out here. Adara grinned at him.

"No, actually. It makes me immune to magic. I'm not sure if that's just hostile magic or all magic. I've never had anybody try to cast a *beneficial* spell on me. But it can't be stolen, can't be removed by anybody but me. You could cut off my head, but then the magic would be destroyed and it would become just a not-very-pretty piece of jewelry."

Fascinated, Stellan undid the laces of Adara's jerkin so he could pull the Darkshield out for another look. The gem gleamed dully in the firelight. "This helped you to defeat the Mancer King?" he asked.

"It hid me, and my mother before me, from him for years," she replied. "He had the ability to use his magical sight to see things thousands of miles away, but I was just a hole in his vision. Yet he had other ways of finding out where I was. That's why I had to track him down and kill him."

This reminder of the deadly side of his lover's nature didn't put Stellan off in the least. If anything, it made him desire her more. He drew her into his arms again, kissing her neck, and squeezed her left breast with his right hand. She reached down with her own right hand, feeling his hardness beneath the soft leather of his trousers. She began rubbing and squeezing, and was about to suggest Stellan bring it out to play, when there was an abrupt alert from Malika: someone coming!

Adara jumped to her feet, startling Stellan. Striding over to the tree against which Voleur rested in its scabbard, she told him "Malika says someone is coming through the woods toward us." Now he was on his feet, drawing the long dagger he still wore at his belt though he'd removed his sword once they were encamped.

Go see, Adara sent to the semigryph, and she slunk off into the woods. They'd made their campsite on the nearest bit of level ground, some fifty feet east of the road. Riding along with Malika, looking out through her eyes with her vastly superior night vision, Adara soon saw that the intruder was approaching on a good-sized, dark-colored horse. The figure looked small… a woman?

With a rueful bark of laughter, Adara returned her sword to its sheath, and stood facing the fire in the direction of the road. Stellan looked at her questioningly. "You can put your knife away," she said. "It's Jaime."

Chapter 14

Sitting beside the morning campfire, Jaime cowered beneath his big sister's glare and gnawed on a hunk of trail bread that was almost too tough to chew while he waited for the porridge to cook. "What are we going to do with you?" Adara sighed. "Truss you up in a sack over Figi's back and slap him on the rump after pointing him in the direction of home? Feed you to the trolls?"

"There's no such thing as trolls," the boy said stubbornly. "And I was out here by myself for two nights without getting eaten by bears or gryphons, too. I know how to take care of myself in the woods. I went out camping plenty of times with Uncle Henrich and Joey."

Adara had to admit, her little step-brother had a point. It was no mean feat for a twelve-year-old to have set out on a journey of more than a hundred miles up into the mountains, and camped by himself in the wilderness for two nights without help. He'd even arrived at their campsite with a pair of half-frozen rabbits hanging from his saddlebow, shot by him during the day's travel up from the main road.

She sighed again. They would lose six days if they accompanied Jaime back to Underhill, probably seven. And it was too late to return him before his parents became alarmed. "Your parents are probably worried sick about you," she pointed out.

The kid actually favored her with a cocky grin! "Nah," he said casually, proud of his skill at subterfuge, "They think I'm up at the Sandersons' for a week-long sleepover. Mama said she and Leana could get by without me at the market stand for the week. It's like a vacation. I think they wanted to throw me a bone, because they felt bad about telling me I couldn't go with you."

Adara was dumfounded. The little weasel! Though she was a long way from becoming a parent herself, and wasn't sure she ever wanted to be one, she felt a stab of sympathy for her mother. The poor woman had already lost *one* child, even if that had eventually worked out all right. "You just told them, 'I'm going to go stay at the neighbors' for a week, see you later,' and they believed it?" she asked.

"Niko Sanderson is my best friend," Jaime explained. "We're like blood brothers. He rode over on his horse and we worked it out for him to tell Mama that his mother wanted to invite me. They have fish in their pond, and their own swimming hole right near the house. It's really great there in summertime."

Adara threw up her hands, stirred the porridge pot, and took it off the fire. She dished out a bowlful and handed it over to her wayward little brother. "You're going to have to face the music sooner or later," she warned, "and you'll probably be banned from hanging around with Niko for the rest of the summer, if not longer. But I guess you can come with us up to Feingeld. I'll need to be convinced the tomb doesn't harbor any threats before I'll let you come down into it with us."

He grinned and said "Thanks, sis!" before tucking into his oatmeal. Meanwhile Stellan had the bedrolls and tent stowed, and was giving the horses some grain before they got started on today's trek. He joined them at the fire for some breakfast. "So we're not going back to Willoughby to turn this miscreant in to the authorities?" he asked cheerfully. The boy's presence had put a damper on his sex life last night, but he had hopes there would be other opportunities soon.

"He'll come with us to the Dunblitz," Adara said. "And once we've inspected the tomb, we'll decide whether he comes any further. I hope there's still an inn up in Feingeld. I'll pay somebody to sit on him while we're gone, if it looks too risky for him to be along on the expedition." There was no hint of the possibility of a situation in which it would be too risky for *her*, or for Stellan, to go inside the fabled tomb.

Jaime had somehow managed to outfit himself well for the trip, especially considering that he'd had to done so in a hurry and in secret. He'd packed plenty of warm clothes, oats for his horse, water skins, trail bread for several days, and even a long dagger that might almost do for a short sword considering his small stature. The three of them with their four horses soon got underway.

They arrived in the once-prosperous town of Feingeld near midday. A handful of its structures still remained, but it had been many centuries since the mountain village's heyday as a trading center. For another couple of centuries after the disappearance of the kobolds the gold deposits that had given the town its name had held out, but now there were not more than a dozen buildings – most of them run-down cabins – still occupied.

The current residents of Feingeld were goat herders and hunters for the most part. Though oddly, the tiny hamlet still boasted an inn of sorts. A small economic niche had been carved out providing services to big game hunters who came to the mountains seeking dragons, gryphons, and other elusive creatures.

The Dragon's Head hunting lodge even had some paying customers at the moment, a member of Northmarch's minor nobility and his party who were staying here for a week searching the mountains for trophies. The innkeeper, who had a hard time making it through the winter most years, was ecstatic. He assured Adara that if they wished to park the boy here for a few days he'd be more than happy to keep an eye on him – for a suitable payment, of course.

They bought a hot meal from him, bowls of the game stew that was kept simmering over the fire in perpetuity, and went on their way. Adara was pretty sure they might be able to reach the Dunblitz today, provided all of the landmarks from a millennium ago were still in existence and the mountain trails had not been erased by avalanches or landslides.

One landmark at least still remained. In the area that had once been the town's broad central plaza, many of the stones were missing – reduced to dust by centuries of expansion and contraction as they were subjected to rain, snow, freezing temperatures, and summer sun. But many others were still intact. And at the center sat a broad circular plaque, probably six inches thick and eight feet across, in the form of a compass rose.

"Holy Baldor, that's irilium!" Stellan gasped after kneeling to inspect it more closely.

"Probably the only reason it's still here is it was too heavy to haul off and sell," Adara opined. The value of such a large quantity of that rare elven metal was high, but perhaps not worth the trouble of digging it up and transporting it to the nearest place where it might be sold.

She had penned a series of notes gleaned from the book she'd found in Carlienne, and Adara now held the paper up and read the first instruction. Luckily, the day was clear for the most part – though many puffy white and gray cumulonimbus clouds cruised above the peaks that surrounded the town on three sides.

Standing in the center of the plaque, Adara counted off the degrees until she was facing just a little east of due northeast. She pulled a small folding spyglass from an inside pocket of her warm cloak and held it to her eye. Yes, there it was – the hulking, dome-topped dark gray bulk of the Dunblitz. It was likely volcanic in origin, the rounded dome of basalt formed in prehistoric times by a slow ooze of lava. Amongst the light gray granite of the rest of the range, the Dunblitz stood out, though it was far shorter than the peaks surrounding it.

"There's the mountain," Adara said, pointing. They mounted up and she led them off to the east, where a goat track wound off in the general direction they wanted to go. Jaime's face was flushed with excitement, thrilled to be going along on this adventure just like he'd wanted. The trouble he was going to be in at home was brushed from his mind like an annoying gnat.

They had to ride single file on the trail, and as Adara was the one leading them Stellan took up a position at the rear. If anything should attack them, he hoped he'd be able to spot it in time to do something about it. Though he doubted they had anything to fear, at least this close to that hunting lodge. Dragons, gryphons, and rocs were so rare and shy it would have been the worst kind of bad luck to meet one. Bears and snow lions were a lot commoner, but the former preferred to hunt at lower elevations and the latter in darkness. Nothing to worry about. He rode with his bow strung, though – as did Adara.

The goat track led to a broad hay meadow, and Adara consulted her list of landmarks before choosing a track that led away from it on the opposite side. The meadow was dotted with goats, and they waved to the goatherd as they rode past him.

They wound among the mountains, picking their way up beside snow-fed rivulets and traversing narrow ledges. Maridem be praised, the weather remained fine. Malika decided to hop down off of

Zarhya's saddle and go hunting up a slope littered with squared-off boulders, using her wings to help her leap from one to the next. Adara watched her in bemusement. She was sure the young semigryph had grown in the days since she'd been rescued. Probably all that red meat Caraline had been feeding her! But the little one seemed the stronger for it.

The three travelers and their horses continued carefully along the narrow path, anxiously aware of the possibility of rockslides. From upslope came a little shriek, and Adara (who had been putting all of her attention into traversing the slope) sent her mind out to see what Malika was doing. Ah, she had caught a cony.

During the summer these little creatures, about the size of a small rabbit, gathered hay and other vegetable matter from the rocky mountain hillsides where they made their dens – enough to last them for the long winter to come. The one Malika had caught was fat and juicy. Come, Adara sent, and the young semigryph picked the cony up in her jaws. Then, climbing atop the boulder in front of her, she opened her wings and launched herself into the air – not so much flying as gliding to land atop Zarhya's saddle. It was a good thing the mare was not skittish!

"Good job, Malika," Adara said aloud, while silently she sent "I'll take it. You can have it back after we get off this slope. Danger!" The semigryph looked at her askance, but relinquished her grip on the dead cony. Adara tied its hind legs together with a length of cord and slung it to rear of the saddle, then directed Zarhya to begin moving forward again.

The Dunblitz grew ever larger, until the travelers were so close to it that it was hard to recognize the mountain's rounded shape. Only the nearly-black stone, so different from the mountains around it, told them they were in the right place. By then the sun was falling toward the western horizon.

Adara guided Zarhya off of the trail they were following, if you could even call it a trail. It was a strip of ground that seemed marginally clearer of large rocks and vegetation than the area surrounding it, and it appeared to lead up the mountain. Off to the east was a sloping meadow, cut through by a small stream coming down off the mountainside.

"I think we'll stop here for the night," she told her companions. "Tomorrow morning we'll search for the air shaft the journal mentioned. If it turns out the tomb is infested with six-foot blind spiders or something, Jaime, we'll be dropping you off back in Feingeld before we take them on." She said it half as a joke, but her brother gave her a sullen look. "Come on," Adara continued, "skin out those bunnies while I get the fire going. Tomorrow, we find the Tomb of the Kobold King!"

Chapter 15

"I think we'd better leave the horses here," Adara said an hour after they'd set out. The trail, if it had ever truly been one, had long since petered out. And the horses were not mountain goats. The Dunblitz' summit was free of snow, the entirety of the rounded peak below the tree line; but little vegetation had been able to take root in the crumbling basalt above this point. Here, at least, there were some grasses growing their mounts could eat, and a trickle of water where they might obtain a drink.

Adara and Stellan were clad in mountaineering boots, but Jaime had brought only one set of footwear – his riding boots, with their slick leather soles. "Jaime, it's too dangerous for you to go rock climbing in those," his big sister told him. "If I'm right about the landmarks, the air shaft should come out in the face of that cleft up there." She gestured to the northwest, where a darker spot in the mountain's southern face marked where the dome had split and partially fallen away.

"But, you said I could come with you into the tomb!" Jaime protested. He hadn't perpetrated the biggest offense against parental authority in his young life and ridden all this way, just to be left behind on the doorstep like some… little kid. "If we find the air shaft, we still have to figure out how to get inside it," Adara pointed out. "We should be back within an hour. Then once we get inside, if it's safe, we'll rope you together with us so you can make it up the slope in those boots. All right?"

Stay with Jaime, Adara sent to Malika as she and Stellan gathered their gear – including walking sticks – and set off up the nearly vertical mountainside in the direction of the cleft. The semigryph had accepted the boy as a member of her family, no doubt associating him with the many delicious meals she'd enjoyed at Underhill. She happily padded over to a patch of meadow grass and wildflowers that was lit by the morning sun and sprawled there, enjoying the warmth. Last night the temperatures had been freezing, and she had insisted on sharing the tent with Adara and Stellan.

Once again Adara was pleased at Stellan's level of competence. Choosing him as a questing companion had proven to be a sound move, and not just for the hot sex. They soon found themselves picking their way across a less-steep stretch on the apron of the cleft, littered with weathered gray-black boulders that had once formed part of the Dunblitz' dome. Ahead, the rock face was in shade and looked black as night.

Puffing, the two pulled up in front of the face. It had not sheared off smoothly, but crumbled irregularly. Down near the bottom of the cut there was a recess maybe ten feet wide and as many high – not a cave, but an indentation no more than six feet deep. Adara supposed if one were caught here in a blizzard, it might provide a modicum of shelter. And within that indentation, they caught the glint of metal.

The hole was roughly circular, and went back into the mountainside too far to see the end. Covering it was not a door, but a grating of crisscrossed metal bars each around an inch in thickness. It appeared they'd been mortared into holes drilled in the rock surrounding the opening.

Stellan seized one and gave a tug, and it shifted slightly. More than a thousand years of freezing and thawing had not been kind to the mortar, even in this sheltered location. "Irilium," he remarked. "The kobolds must have had access to a big lode of ore."

Adara nodded. "They were probably the most skilled miners Eorla has ever known," she said. "Tunneling through rock was something they were born to, so it was no wonder they mastered the skills of smelting and smithing to go along with all of the ore they must have found."

"I was kind of expecting a door of some kind," Stellan admitted. "What's with this grate?" Adara smiled at him. "The kobolds didn't need a door into the tomb up here," she explained. "They tunneled up from beneath to create their 'high up' resting place for the king. But they breathed air just like the rest of us. They had to bore an air shaft to let air circulate through the spaces below."

Stellan considered. "Huh, good thing I suppose. It would have been a bit of a problem to get into the tomb and discover there was no air. Well, I guess we just need to get these bars out." Adara glanced back the way they had come. She could just make out the meadow where they'd left the horses, a quarter of a mile away.

"It's a pity we can't bring one of the horses up that slope," she said. "We could just tie ropes to the bars and Sadiq could pull them loose."

"I don't think that will be necessary," Stellan said confidently. He pulled a five-pound, short-shafted hammer and a steel masonry chisel from the pack he'd set on the ground.

"Better have some eye protection," Adara reminded him, and he brought forth a pair of leather goggles with thick glass set into them. The glass was protected by metal screening, making him look like some kind of fantastic insect as he set the chisel to the end of one of the bars and began whaling on it with the hammer.

Adara stood off a way, watching as he worked. The hole was no more than four feet in diameter, and there was not room for two to perform this task. He possessed much more arm strength than she did – something her Learning Ring could not overcome, alas – so it fell to him to chip away at the bars' attachments until they came loose.

Again Adara considered enlisting the aid of Nomen, and decided against it. The earth elemental could probably have fractured the rock holding the bars in a few seconds, saving them hours of hard labor; but he might also bring half the mountain down on them. She paced around the ledge, anxious, as Stellan worked methodically away on the bars' attachments. "This mortar is pretty rotten," he announced cheerfully, freeing both ends of a bar and sliding it out after no more than ten minutes.

Not all of them were that easy, but most came out without too much trouble. Stellan handed each free bar to Adara, and she lovingly stacked them over to one side of the ledge near their packs. They represented a considerable treasure in and of themselves, and much more portable than the compass disk had been.

"You should leave the bottom two cross-bars in place," Adara pointed out as Stellan was about to begin on one of them. He looked up at her questioningly. "I'm pretty sure that tunnel leads to a straight shaft leading down," she said. "We can attach our ropes to the cross-bars."

He slapped his forehead, grinning wryly, and said "Right. I forgot."

Within two hours all but the upright bars immediately to the left and right of the circular opening, and the bottom two crosswise bars, had been removed and neatly stacked. Adara couldn't resist going inside, enlisting the fire elemental Salomand's aid in lighting one of the torches they'd brought, and walking bent over down the tunnel to see how far it went into the mountain. Stellan, who'd done all the work since they got here, was as eager as she was – but the quarters inside that tunnel were cramped. He stayed outside, taking pulls from a water skin.

A minute or so later Adara returned, snuffing her torch by calling on Ariel to withdraw the air from around it. Stellan raised an eyebrow. "Neat trick," he remarked, and she smiled.

"The tunnel only goes in around twenty-five feet, and the vertical shaft is the same diameter. It's hard to tell how far down it goes, but probably not much more than fifty feet. And there's a blue glow coming up from the bottom of it!"

"That must be the phorium you told me about," Stellan said. The crystalline mineral, mined from the rocks deep below the Ratskells, had a natural glow bright enough for the kobolds to see by – if it might be a little dim for human eyes. They had used it for lighting in their underground homes, and sometimes traded it to humans who found it an interesting curiosity.

He enfolded Adara in a dusty hug, and kissed her on the lips. "We're almost there, baby!" he crowed. "But I'm starving. What's for lunch?" She kissed him back, and pretended she was a tavern wench.

"We have the trail bread stew, or if you prefer there's the filet of trail bread garni in trail bread sauce… with a side of trail bread."

Stellan went along with it, frowning in concentration and holding up a finger. "I think I'll have… the trail bread!" he declared. Then he looked around him. "Let's leave the rest of this stuff here, but bring one of the rope coils." They also took along their hiking sticks, and when they got to the edge of the gently sloping ledge they selected a wagon-sized boulder to tie their rope to. It provided an aid for getting down (and back up) the steep slope below.

They arrived at their impromptu camp to a remarkable sight. Jaime, bored with waiting, had stuffed one of a pair of heavy red

woolen socks into its mate, and was playing a game with Malika –
throwing the fuzzy bolus up into the air. The semigryph launched
herself upward with powerful hindquarters and her wings, snatching
it out of the air on its downward trajectory and then fluttering to a
landing to give it back to him for another throw.

Malika immediately became aware of Adara's arrival and
abandoned the game, and Jaime turned quickly to see them walking
into camp. "About time!" he said. "Hey, did you see what I taught
Mali to do?" Adara grinned and hugged him.

"That's great, Jaime!" she said with genuine enthusiasm. This
sort of play was exactly what the half-grown kit needed to strengthen
her injured wing and become the aerial hunter nature had intended
her to be.

"So, did you find it?" Jaime asked. He couldn't imagine they
would have been gone so long, otherwise.

"We found it," Adara said with a smile, "and Stellan got the bars
off the opening so we can go inside. We just need to eat some lunch
and gather up the rest of our gear, then we'll be ready to descend the
shaft and see what's down there."

The boy's eyes widened with delight. "Can I come?" he asked
eagerly. Adara and Stellan exchanged glances. She nodded. "We
rigged a rope for the steep part of the slope, so you should be able to
climb it without too much trouble. You're not getting let down the
shaft until I'm sure nothing is waiting to attack us at the bottom, but I
guess you and Malika can come up and be there while I do the initial
exploration."

"Uh, what about the horses?" Jaime asked.

"We'll take off their saddles and bridles," Stellan said. "They've
got good grazing here, and I don't think they're going to wander off.
We'll only be down for a few hours at a time, anyhow, and back here
before nightfall so we can protect them from snow lions if there are
any." Snow lions were considerably smaller than their warm-climate
cousins, more likely to attack prey the size of goats.

The boy swiftly dismissed his concerns, and they all fell to
eating their trail bread repast with as much enthusiasm as could be
mustered. It wasn't that the stuff tasted bad… it just got monotonous
after a few meals in a row. They left some of their food and camp

supplies behind, but almost all the rest of the gear and their packs, including Sadiq's load, came up the mountainside with them.

Jaime's eyes got big when he saw the opening in the rock face, the glistening bars piled to one side. "Is this irilium?" he asked, and Stellan nodded. The metal was prized for its light weight, strength, and resistance to oxidation for more applications than arms and armor. If it were less rare and easier to work, many everyday implements would be made of the stuff.

There was a brief discussion between Adara and Ferdyn as to who was going to be first down the vertical shaft. "It'll be a lot easier for you to pull *me* back up in a hurry than the other way around, " Adara pointed out.

"But…" Stellan didn't really have an answer to that, but he didn't like the idea of dropping his lover into the bowels of the earth where almost anything might be waiting for her.

"All right," Adara said finally. "Just for you, Stellan my love, I will put on my armor before going down there." She rustled in her pack and dug out her set of irilium plate: helmet, hauberk, greaves, and vambraces. She stripped down to her underwear, unconcerned by Jaime's presence, and then put on the suit of under-padding that prevented the plate from digging into her flesh.

"Give me a hand with this, will you dear?" Adara beckoned to Stellan. The part of the armor covering her torso was designed so she could get into it by herself, but she needed help with the vambraces. His eyes were wide as he fastened the straps for her. This suit of armor, perfectly fitted to her form by a master smith with the closely guarded skills of the merudur, might have cost the full amount he had stolen from the duke's treasury five years back. Clearly, though they had gotten past their reserve enough to reveal some secrets to each other, she still had more to tell.

Adara had designed this armor herself. She wasn't planning on going into battle against knights wielding lances, but had wanted something that would protect her vital areas while still allowing her to move freely – on foot or in the saddle. Part of her upper arms and her elbows were left bare, protected only by the cloth-and-leather padding. Her knees and lower legs were similarly not armored, though the high leather boots offered some protection. She wore reinforced, fingerless leather gloves on her hands, allowing her to strap on the irilium helmet without assistance.

Jaime was gazing at her in awe. He'd been pretty well convinced that his new-found big sister was a hero out of legend since the day she'd first appeared in his life, and this latest evidence only confirmed it. With her dagger at her side (and a few smaller ones for throwing, a skill she'd learned from Ferdyn, secreted about her person), Voleur on her back, Adara looked ready to take on a demon army single-handed. Though in fact, she had yet to kill anyone with that lethal-looking blade.

They tied two of their several lengths of rope to the upper crossbar at the entrance to the horizontal shaft. One was tied in a loop around her waist, the other allowed to dangle down the shaft. Adara had some torches and a few other items she might need in a sack dangling from her buckler, but she thought that the glow from the phorium should provide enough light for her descent. Seizing the dangling rope in both hands and stepping out into the vertical shaft, she told Stellan "All right. Start lowering me down. I'll let you know if I need a quick return trip." She winked at him, but his expression was serious.

Holding tight to the rope with her gloved hands, Adara walked her way down the shaft. It was not as deep as she'd thought, seeming to run no more than five times her own height before she abruptly stepped out into air and began swaying, held by her grip on the dangling rope as well as by the other around her waist. "I've reached the end of the shaft!" she called up to Stellan, silhouetted against the torchlight in the horizontal shaft not thirty feet above her. He stopped lowering her, and she peered down. The part of the armor that protected her torso also protected her neck and throat with a high collar, which made bending her head downward very far something of a trick.

She was in a broad cavern, roughly oval in shape. The air shaft had been cut into the center, which was the high point of the ceiling at perhaps twenty feet above the stone floor. And it was a lot brighter in here than she'd expected. It seemed that the native basalt of the mountain forming the inside of the chamber had been almost completely tiled in slices of phorium. Wow!

Hanging there, swaying gently, Adara looked around carefully. It were better to find out about the six-foot blind spiders from here, rather than discovering them after she'd landed. In the blue glow, to which her eyes were rapidly becoming accustomed, she saw no signs of movement. The space was broken up with some black pillars, left to help support the shallowly domed ceiling, and she could see that there were artifacts scattered around – most of them over toward the side nearest the mountain's heart.

"Go ahead and lower me down the rest of the way," Adara called up. "It's about twenty feet!"

"Take care!" Stellan called down, and began slowly paying out the rope until she alit on the smooth, glowing blue floor. She peered up the shaft, barely able to make out Stellan's form at the top.

"I'm good!" she called. "I'm going to untie the rope, but hang onto it until I tell you!"

"Will do!" he called back.

After untying the rope from around her waist, Adara stood in the center of the chamber and slowly spun through a full circle. Over there near what she thought of as the "inner" wall, she saw a gaping black hole. A shaft going down, the one the ancient kobolds had dug before excavating this chamber, she guessed. She hadn't come equipped for a full expedition, but perhaps on a later trip she and Stellan could explore the entire complex – maybe even find the secret exit the kobold traders had used when taking their goods to places like Feingeld.

Except for that one subterranean entrance, and the air shaft above her head, there were no openings in the glowing blue walls. They had not bothered to cover the support pillars, but every other surface of the chamber's interior had been tiled in the translucent, glowing blue stone. The effect was breathtakingly beautiful.

Spaced at intervals around the walls on the "outer" side of the chamber were waist-high carved white stone pillars – or at least Adara thought they were white. It was hard to tell in this blue light. She was reluctant to spoil the effect, but pulled out one of her torches and requested Salomand's help to light it. From the way it flared, she could see that there was a fairly good air current running from the distant opening and up the shaft.

Yes, the pillars were white. Each of them had some artifact sitting atop it, and an etched metal plaque with unfamiliar runes on it. No doubt telling those who could read them what the artifacts were, and their history. Wow. Oh, if only there were a living kobold scholar to translate those for her! She could write a detailed history of that lost people, one that would dazzle the world. Of course, if there *were* a kobold scholar, they wouldn't be a lost people and the history wouldn't be nearly so important.

Perhaps, somewhere in the Royal Library in Carlienne (where she'd obtained the information that had brought her to this place), Adara might find a means to translate those runes into modern Franca. She walked back toward the other side of the chamber, passing the air shaft. There was a litter of dirt, dust, pebbles, dead insects, and the bones of small creatures in that area.

"Hey, everything all right?" Stellan called down anxiously.

"No giant spiders," Adara reported. "But these trolls are a nuisance! Just wait until I dispatch them, then you can sent Jaime down to see."

"Ha ha, very funny," came the reply. She felt a little guilty about keeping her companions on tenterhooks, and hurried over to the inner side of the room where the largest collection of artifacts was displayed.

Up against the far wall, some forty feet from the tunnel presumed to be leading down to lower levels, was a broad and tall platform made of that same white stone. Atop it sat an irilium sarcophagus. The lid was above Adara's eye level, but she guessed it had been molded into an image of the coffin's inhabitant.

The space around the catafalque had been cordoned off by a carved stone balustrade, and within that fenced-off area more treasures were displayed. There were axes, swords, and daggers forged from irilium, their hafts worked in gold and studded with gems. A full set of irilium armor, far more elaborate than Adara's own, was mounted on a stone statue. Surely, this must be the great king's own armor – worn by his carven likeness. The armor covered almost everything from head to toe, but it was clear he had been a little shorter than Adara and at least twice as wide.

And there were chests – massive things, made all of metal. What treasures might these contain? Adara could hardly wait to find out. But first, she had better invite the rest of her party to come down. She went back to the shaft. "Nobody down here but us tomb raiders," she called up cheerfully to Stellan. "Why don't you truss Jaime up and send him down?"

She heard a muted "Yeah!" from the boy, as the rope she'd left dangling was hauled up. A minute or two later he came down the shaft, swinging from side to side, like a fat spider on a silken thread. He had not held onto the stationary rope as Adara had – because he had Malika wrapped in his arms.

Adara was standing at the bottom of the shaft ready to catch him, and gave a startled oath as the semigryph took to the air and glided down to the floor as soon as she and Jaime had cleared the shaft. "Why on earth did you bring *her*?" Adara asked in exasperation.

"I couldn't just leave her," the boy protested. "She wanted to come!"

Adara shook her head. When going back up they'd just have to have Jaime carry Malika in his arms again as he was hauled up by Stellan. The shaft was vertical, and not nearly wide enough for her to fly up even if she could get off the ground. "Send down my pack too, will you?" she called up after Jaime had been untied. It was soon lowered to her.

Next Stellan came down the dangling rope quickly, walking himself down the shaft wall and then using hands and feet to descend from the ceiling before dropping the last six feet to land gracefully, knees bent. He had not bothered to put on any armor, but he was wearing his sword and dagger and had brought along his own pack – the more capacious one they'd bought in Willoughby. His dark eyes glittered in the blue light as he gazed around the chamber.

"Wow, it's real!" Jaime said in awe, spinning as he tried to take in everything at once.

"I get the idea this was almost more like a museum or a memorial than a tomb," Adara said. "There are plaques on all those pillars over there, and another big one over in front of where the king's body is lying. I'll bet kobolds would come here like it was a pilgrimage, to look at the greatest treasures of their race and remember their great king and his deeds."

"A pity we can't read the plaques," Stellan said. But Adara could tell that learning more about the kobolds was not foremost in his mind. He had been drawn like a moth to a flame, and was now gazing at the treasures on display around the king's sarcophagus.

"Did you bring paper and charcoal?" Adara asked him, and he unslung the pack from his back. He handed over a roll of paper, and a muslin bag in which were several sticks of charcoal for drawing. "I'm going to take some rubbings from those plaques against the far wall," she told him.

"And I'm going to see what's in those chests!" he replied, hopping over the balustrade.

Malika was padding around the space, seemingly a little freaked out by the glowing floor. She sniffed at the remains of rodents that had died before her ancestors had been born, and then gravitated toward the dark tunnel on the far side of the room. Stay with me, Adara sent. She didn't want to divide her attention between what she was doing and the semigryph's investigation. And just because the kobolds were gone, didn't mean there wasn't something else living down here. Best they leave that tunnel undisturbed until they were ready to do a full-fledged exploration.

Stellan found the chests locked, as he'd expected. He pulled out his lockpicks, the finest set money could buy, and stooped to begin working at a keyhole. The ancient kobolds had been possibly the greatest metalworkers Q'ur had ever known, and their skill with intricate mechanisms had been superb. Adara had finished taking rubbings of five of the plaques and was starting on the sixth before he heard a final "click" and the latch opened.

He pushed the heavy lid up, breath held. Would it be full to the top with gold, gems, exquisite jewelry? Or perhaps the mortal remains of the late king's wives? He'd read that some ancient kings had been interred with their entire courts, ensuring a clean and thorough transition from one ruler to the next.

Scrolls. The tightly sealed metal chest, lined with cedar wood, was full up to the top with scrolls! Stellan sighed in frustration. Here was the historic treasure Adara had sought, assuming some way could be found to read the runes of the ancient kobolds. It occurred to him that for the underground-dwelling kobolds, the wood lining the chest and the paper on which the scrolls had been written was as rare and valuable as those iridium weapons were to him. Certainly, there were not many trees to be found growing in the bowels of the earth!

He recalled that Adara had said this place might have been intended for living kobolds to visit and behold their race's greatest king and his treasures. In that case, it wouldn't have made a lot of sense to fill up locked chests with gold and gems – who would see them? And this arrangement suggested that the kobolds were *not* among the cultures of Q'ur that believed burying the dead with their physical possessions assured that they would carry these things into the afterlife.

Adara is really starting to affect my mind, Stellan mused. Here he was thinking about the kobolds from a scholarly perspective, not stuffing his pockets with everything that looked valuable. Steeling himself to find another treasure trove of unreadable historical documents, he crouched to begin picking the lock on the second chest.

Meanwhile Jaime, who'd just been staring at everything, finally worked up the courage to pick up a leaf-bladed irilium short sword with a jeweled pommel. It was so beautiful, yet so menacing. He knew from the history he'd been forced to study that most "real" weapons were plain and unadorned – tools for killing and nothing more. But he had no difficulty imagining that this sword, despite its ornate beauty, could cut through your enemies like a scythe through grain.

Taking the fencing posture he'd been taught, Jaime held the short sword out and began pretending he was fighting an opponent, marveling at the way the blue light suffusing the chamber glittered off the polished blade as he turned it from side to side. "Hah! Take that! En garde!" he grunted in an undertone, really getting into it.

Concentrating on the lock he was trying to tease open, Stellan smiled to himself. He well recalled what it was like to be a twelve-year-old boy. Though he, as a member of the nobility, had been trained by a professional fencing master from the age of ten. He looked up in alarm as the sword suddenly clanged on the stone floor.

Across the room, Adara dropped the paper and charcoal she was holding as she heard the sword hit the stones. At the same instant Malika, who'd been huddling near to her side, suddenly turned hissing – fur on end and wings slightly spread – and sent "Strangers!" Stellan was on his feet, drawing his sword, as Jaime stood paralyzed in shock. From the dark opening a few feet away, a troop of short, broad, gray-skinned warriors – dressed in a motley assortment of armor and wielding swords and spears – hustled into the room and spread out to pen the intruders within the stone fence surrounding the catafalque. They had not yet spotted Adara.

One of them spoke, astonishingly in heavily-accented Franca: "Put down sword, hu-man!" Jaime was struggling not to wet his pants, no threat to anyone despite the dagger he wore at his belt. But Stellan wasn't going to let a little thing like being outnumbered twenty to one stop him. He lifted his sword, dagger in the other hand, and made to leap over the balustrade. Just then, the warriors parted to reveal a smaller man, ancient-looking but still powerfully muscled, carrying an irilium staff with a gem mounted in its top.

He pointed it at Stellan, who collapsed bonelessly to the floor – sword and dagger falling from his limp hands. Next he gestured to Jaime, dropping the lad where he stood. Adara had Voleur out of its sheath, and she called Salomand to her aid. But as fire sprang up among the troop of warriors, it found no purchase. Their clothing was metal, their hides tough, and they were hairless and beardless as well.

Oh, shit. Adara was good with that blade, but she didn't see how she was going to be able to bring down more than a dozen bull-like warriors only a little shorter than she was – especially the ones with spears. As she hesitated, she felt the Darkshield grow warm. It pulsed blue for a moment, though it was hidden inside her armor and no one saw it.

Brandishing Voleur, Adara began stalking toward the warriors. Could she bluff them into running, realizing that the spells their magus or whatever he was had cast had no effect on her? The man with the staff barked an order in a language that was *not* Franca, and

101

in another second the one who'd told Stellan to put down his sword had leapt over the balustrade and was holding a dagger to Jaime's throat.

"Surrender or I kill him," he told her. "And the other too." Adara sagged. She re-sheathed her sword and looked around to see Malika cowering, growling low in her throat, behind her. It's all right, don't fear, she sent, and the semigryph quieted. Her fur and feathers were still fluffed out, though. "I give up, don't hurt us," she said. The long-lost kobolds, it seemed, had just been found.

Chapter 16

Adara stumbled, barely managing to stop herself from sprawling face down on the stone floor of the tunnel with her hands tied behind her back. They had stripped her of her sword, dagger, and armor, but had missed the two daggers hidden in her boots. For all the good that would do her against nearly two dozen kobold warriors, who looked as if they could pick her up in one hand though she overtopped them by inches.

They'd been moving for hours now, winding ever downward through a labyrinth of tunnels carved in black stone. Adara was tired, hungry, and thirsty, and she worried about how Jaime was faring. She could barely see him in the dim light from occasional clusters of phorium crystals, mounted in the tunnel walls at intervals of around twenty feet.

The kobold with the staff had evidently reversed his spell of paralysis on Stellan and Jaime after the two had been relieved of their weapons and their hands bound. Then he and his troop of warriors had engaged in a discussion in their own language before hustling the captives out of the tomb. The kobolds had not known what to make of Malika, but Adara had promised the semigryph would stay by her side and cause no trouble.

No further words had been spoken in Franca, and Adara had no idea where they were going or why. But it appeared their captors didn't intend to kill them out of hand, at least. How fortunate, she thought, that they had not actually been in the act of plundering the kobold king's treasures when they were surprised.

Ahead of her Jaime sagged, then fell to his knees. "I can't... go on," he groaned.

"Get my brother some water!" Adara demanded. "He's only a child!" The staff-wielder, who was up at the head of the group, growled a command to the kobolds flanking the boy, and one of them produced a water skin from his belt and held it to Jaime's mouth so he could drink.

All halted until the boy was on his feet again. To Adara's astonishment the old leader rasped, "Apologies. We are almost there." Wherever "there" was, she was glad to hear it. Fifteen minutes later they came to a stretch of tunnel barred by a rune-carved door of black metal, which the leader opened, so it seemed, by casting a spell with his staff.

Beyond the door was a larger space, somewhat better lit, with many doorways leading off of it. Some of them had doors on them, most did not. More commands were issued, and Stellan and Jaime were put into a chamber with a locked door. Two of the kobold warriors took up station outside it, while the two escorting Adara hustled her along to another chamber – this one without a door.

There were considerably more of the phorium crystals here, and Adara was able to see that the room – maybe fifteen by twenty feet in size – held only a stone table and two stone chairs. There was no fireplace in the room, but the temperature was comfortable enough – dressed as she was in her cloth-and-leather armor padding. The room felt stark without any carpet or wall hangings, but she guessed that any it might once have held would have rotted away centuries ago.

Adara's captors beckoned her to sit in one of the chairs, while the old kobold with the staff took the other. He then dismissed the rest of the troop – though she noticed that two of them had remained on either side of the doorway. She sat eyeing the kobold magic user curiously, glad to be off her feet.

Cruztan Milegos' theory that the kobolds were a race of elves seemed borne out by their appearance. They were constructed like any human, with two arms attached to hands having four fingers and a thumb each, two legs (presumably with five-toed feet, though these were hidden), and so forth.

Adara had seen merudur in Carlienne and they had been tall and willowy with fine pale hair on their heads; but the kobolds were completely hairless. They were similar to the Swinzen in height and heavily muscled build, but their arms were of a proportionate length for their bodies similar to what you would see in humans. In the blue light it was hard to tell, but their skin seemed to be a pale gray in color.

The enormous eyes, like a cat's with only the irises showing, were pale blue and without lashes. The points of the ears rose slightly above the domes of their round, blunt-featured heads. In the case of the kobold before her, the gray skin was lined with a network of fine wrinkles, suggesting great age. His costume was not so much armor as a sort of calf-length robe made of what looked like ultra-fine irilium chain mail. It draped like fabric.

As she was studying her captor, so he was peering at Adara with as much interest. Finally it was he who spoke. "It is long since I saw one of your blood, hu-man. You are female?" Gee, thanks for noticing, she thought snarkily. Of course with her height and slender build, there were probably some members of her *own* race that would have trouble figuring it out – dressed as she was. Stellan hadn't had any problems with that, though. She stifled a sigh.

"I am," Adara replied shortly. "My name is Adara Willoughby, and I came here to learn of your people. We had believed your kind to be extinct." To her surprise, the old magus cracked a smile and barked a short laugh.

"Extinct! We have been absent from the world above for a mere seven hundred years! I had already counted a thousand years, when last I met with you hu-mans."

Adara had known that the elven races lived a lot longer than did humans. But this guy was saying he was 1700 years old? The kobolds didn't need to study history, they had lived it! "Might I know your name, old one?" she asked respectfully.

"I am Ghryzindion, shaman of the Karindas tribe," he said formally. "Once I was a trader, and learned your tongue. But after the disaster that befell the Karindi, I took on the staff from she who went before me."

A shaman, Adara thought. She didn't know that much about magic, but as she understood it most spells functioned by calling on powers from the spirit world. The differences among witches, magi, sorcerers, and shamans might probably be determined by the nature of the spirits who aided them. The fact that she was sitting here in what she imagined passed for a comfortable chamber, having an intimate chat with Ghryzindion, probably meant they *hadn't* been arrested for desecrating the great king's tomb with their presence.

"What is it that you want from me, Ghryzindion?" Adara asked. It was nice to be sitting down, but she was still tired and hungry and thirsty – and emotionally wrung out from the events of the day. She was anxious to get to the heart of the matter.

The old shaman smiled again. His teeth were large, square, and looked hard enough to chew rocks. "So impatient, you hu-mans," he said. "But I suppose if you think seven hundred years is a long time, you have reason to be. I must know what magic you possess, that you were able to resist my spell of paralysis. And in spite of this you allowed yourself and your companions to be captured."

Uh, oh. Once again Adara found herself in the presence of a powerful magic user with a strong interest in her necklace. Better explain quickly, especially the part about how it couldn't be taken from her by force. She undid the top of her padded suit, revealing the Darkshield.

"The Royal Magus of Tanar called it the Darkshield," she explained. "It has been passed from mother to daughter in my family for many generations – though not for quite so long as *you* have been alive, Old One. It cannot be taken from its wearer by force, and should the wearer die while wearing it its magic will be ended."

The old kobold leaned forward, peering at it with his enormous eyes. In this dim light, it was scarcely more than a black line against Adara's pale skin. "A useful thing," he said slowly. "Though clearly, it does not make you invincible…"

"Aw, I could have taken a few of you if you hadn't threatened to cut my little brother's throat," she replied with an edge of pique. The shaman's air of amused superiority was beginning to get to her.

He sat back in his stone chair. "I meant no offense," he said softly. "In truth, I am hoping to enlist your aid." Huh. It was hard to imagine what help she, a teenage girl, could offer to this ancient and powerful being and his well-armed (and presumably, *very* well-seasoned) band of warriors. But if he wanted her help, there was going to be some reciprocation.

"Did you bring our belongings along?" she asked. She had been midway in the column, and had not seen what was happening behind her during the hours they'd been traveling down into the Dunblitz' depths. Ghryzindion nodded.

"We took all that did not belong within the Memorial Chamber," he replied.

"We have food with us," Adara explained. "Food that will probably suit us better than whatever you people eat. I want food and water brought to me and my companions, and some time to rest. After we have refreshed ourselves, I will hear what it is you wish me to do."

Chapter 17

Adara was shut into the room with Stellan and Jaime – and their packs, which had been inspected for weapons first, were tossed in after her. There was no table in the room, but it had a long stone bench at either end that might once have served as a sleeping platform. Jaime was sprawled out on one, Stellan sitting with his face in his hands on the other. When the door opened and Adara was escorted in, he jumped to his feet with a look of manic relief.

He smothered her in a bear hug, murmuring "Thank Maridem! I thought they'd decided to… I don't know what. But I'm glad you're all right!" Adara hugged him back, and planted a deep kiss on his mouth. After making love half a dozen times a day since they had first come together in that little stream, their love life had been bone dry for going on three days now. She ached for him, never mind their situation.

From the feel of Stellan's body pressed against hers, those thoughts had been passing through his mind as well. Ah, hell. Malika followed Adara in and curled up in a corner of the floor, looking listless. The packs having been deposited inside, the door was closed again. Shortly both of them were digging out trail bread and water skins. The much-denigrated food bars were beginning to seem a lot more desirable.

Adara brought some over to Jaime. He was not sleeping, it seemed, but lying in a depressed and exhausted funk. No wonder, the poor kid. Their adventure had gone from joyful excitement to nightmare in the blink of an eye, and his heroes had *not* been able to save the day.

"Cheer up, little brother," Adara told him matter-of-factly, handing over the food and water. "The kobold shaman says he wants our help, so probably they're going to let us go. Eat some food, and I'm sure you'll feel better." Jaime heaved himself up into a sitting position and fell on the trail bread like a rabid weasel. It looked like he was going to pull through.

Adara and Stellan sat side by side on the opposite bench, talking quietly together. "I've got two daggers they didn't find," she murmured into his ear.

"I've got four," he replied. They both knew such armament wasn't going to buy their way out of here. At this point, had all the kobolds suddenly dropped dead, they would still probably have been wandering down here, lost, until they had all starved to death or died of thirst.

"I demanded we get food and water before I listened to the shaman's proposal," Adara went on. "And some rest. I don't have any idea what time it is out there on the mountainside, but it feels like days since I slept." Stellan squeezed her thigh sympathetically. Then suddenly he stiffened.

"Shit, the horses!" he exclaimed, and her heart sank. She'd been so caught up with worrying over their own problems, she hadn't considered that their mounts had been abandoned in a high mountain meadow with no one to look after them.

"Maybe once the grain is gone they'll decide to go back down the mountain," Adara said hopefully. "If they stay together, they ought to be safe from most of the predators in these parts." He squeezed her thigh again. There was nothing either of them could do about it, but hope for the best.

Their tent and bedrolls had been among the items left in the mountain campsite. But their warm cloaks were in the packs. They spread one atop the other, making at least a little padding on the stone bench, and lay down together with Stellan curled around Adara's back – his left arm cradling her body. She hadn't expected to be able to sleep, between the hard stone bench and her mental turmoil; but within minutes both of them dozed off. It had been a long, tiring day.

Chapter 18

Adara's bladder woke her, and she wriggled out from under Stellan's arm and sat up. Their captors had not provided them with a chamber pot. Good grief, surely kobolds must need to relieve themselves the same as humans? The door was locked, and she pounded on it. "Hey, I need to pee!"

She heard a rattling of the lock, and the door opened. One of the guards on the door was the one who'd spoken in Franca when they were first captured, though his command of the tongue was not as good as Ghryzindion's. "I need to relieve myself," Adara told him, using hand gestures to get her meaning across. His pale blue eyes widened, and he barked a command to his companion. Shortly a handsome metal vessel was brought and handed over, the door closed again.

It occurred to Adara as she squatted over the pot, trying to ignore the lack of privacy, that this group of kobolds might not have dealt with any captives ever before. Perhaps she should cut them a little slack if the accommodations weren't up to her standards.

Stellan and Jaime used the newly provided receptacle as well, and a few minutes later guards came to escort Adara back to the room where she'd interviewed the shaman. "I want my companion to come with me," she told them. To Jaime, she said "I'm hoping to use Stellan to back me up in negotiating with these characters. Try to get some rest while we're gone."

Adara had expected an argument from their captors about bringing Stellan. After all, she was the prisoner here. But it seemed Ghryzindion had told his cohorts that it was important for them to obtain her help. They not only included Stellan in the trip down the hall, but fetched another stone chair and placed it beside the one Adara had occupied earlier. The old shaman sat awaiting them.

"Thank you for allowing us some food and rest," Adara told him politely. "My companion Stellan and I are now ready to hear you out." Ghryzindion eyed the young man curiously.

"Are you a *pomatka*...a breeding female?" he asked Adara. She was taken aback. "I am a young woman, capable of bearing children," she said, not sure what he was getting at. "But I have not borne any."

"Ah, apologies," the old shaman said. "I see that it is much different with hu-mans than with the Kier Ludzi." At Adara's questioning look, he added "The people of the heart, that is, the heart of the world. It is what we whom you call 'kobolds' call ourselves." She nodded.

"I need to explain to you how it is with us, so that you can understand the calamity that befell our people seven hundred years ago," Ghryzindion went on. His audience was rapt. "Among us, as it is with the other long-lived races, births are few. But whereas in most races of the udur any female may become a mother – and most will, though usually only once in a lifespan that can last two millennia – among the Kier Ludzi it is otherwise."

"Some women of my race may bear ten or more children," Adara put in. The old shaman shook his head.

"No doubt your gods intended it as a compensation for your short lives," he remarked. "In any case, as I was trying to explain, in my people around half of all babies born are female. But of these, most are infertile. They look little different from males, save that they lack penises. But one in perhaps one hundred fifty baby girls will be born a pomatka, a brood mother."

"That sounds like bees," Adara murmured in an aside to Stellan, but Ghryzindion's ears were sharp.

"What are these bees you speak of?" he asked curiously.

"Small flying creatures no bigger than the tip of my thumb," she explained. "Most are born female but do not breed. The breeding females are mated by the few males, then rule over the hive being fed and cared for as they lay eggs to keep the colony supplied with new workers."

"What a thing," the old shaman said, astonished. "Indeed, the way our gods made us is very similar. Though any male might become fertile if in contact with a mature pomatka. The brood mother will mate with her consort every five years or so, bearing a single child and nursing it. Once nursing is done, the children are raised by the tribe as a whole."

"Your tribes must be very tightly knit," Adara remarked. Talk about communalism! And over the centuries, they must also be very closely related to each other. "Don't you have problems with… I mean, would not the consort be the queen's brother?"

"No," the old kobold replied. "It is forbidden by our customs for a queen to take a consort from within the tribe. If a consort died or was set aside, or if a new queen reached maturity and needed a consort, one would be sought from among the other tribes."

"So there could be more than one queen for a tribe?" Adara asked. She knew that if two queens arose in a bee colony, they would fight each other to the death. But kobolds were sentient humanoids, not bugs. Ghryzindion shook his head.

"Bearing a fetus that will become a pomatka triggers a change in the pomatka's body," he explained. "By the time the girl reaches sexual maturity, at the age of two hundred years or so, the mother will have lost her fertility. That fertility declines gradually over the centuries, but is completely gone usually a decade or two before the flowering of her daughter."

Huh, fascinating. Adara was thankful she had eaten and rested, else she might have been too impatient for him to get to the point. "And the pomatka is your tribal leader, your political queen as well as the mother of her people?"

"That's right," the old shaman replied. "She will hand over rule to her daughter, whom alone of all her children she will have raised herself, in a ceremony that is celebrated upon the daughter's first flowering."

"Thank you for sharing this information, Ghryzindion," Adara said sincerely. "I truly did not intend any disrespect to your ancient king, but had gone into his tomb seeking to learn more about the, uh… Kier Ludzi. Being able to find out from a living member of your race is so much better!" He smiled graciously at her. "Is your little band all that remains of your people, then?" she went on.

"I was getting to that," the old one said sadly. "These twenty individuals, eleven males including myself and nine freemartins, are all that remain of the Karindas tribe. This complex was once our home, and for thousands of years we thrived here – venturing above ground to trade with the hu-mans at Feingeld and interacting with the other tribes at our gathering grounds beneath the mountains."

"There were many such tribes?" Adara asked. Stellan was as fascinated as she was at what the old kobold had to say, but rather than interject himself into the conversation he was enjoying watching her work. She possessed a way of interacting with others that he was in awe of.

"Were, and are," Ghryzindion said sadly. "It is said that the gods of the Kier Ludzi made us here within these mountains when they created the mountains themselves, forming us from the same gray stone and breathing life into us so that we might have minds and worship them. So far as I know, our people live nowhere else in the world but here within the range of the Szariztin, what you call the Ratskell Mountains. And scattered around this area of a few thousand square miles were thirty small tribes of the Kier Ludzi – each with its own queen."

Adara's blue eyes were wide. She'd had no idea the kobolds had been so numerous. "You said 'are'?" she asked. "If the tribes yet exist, why did they stop trading with us?"

"It was not by their choice," Ghryzindion explained. "And now we are coming to the crux, that with which I need your help."

Adara and Stellan watched him intently. "We are not the only race of udur living beneath the Szariztin," the old kobold began. "There is another people, less numerous than the Kier Ludzi. In ancient times men knew them as the aurudur, the Golden Elves. But they call themselves the Siiri."

His listeners blinked. Adara had found no mention of any such people in any of her researches, though information about the kobolds had been plentiful. "The Siiri are of a height with the Kier Ludzi but where we are as strong as the bones of the earth they are slender, graceful. Their people and ours traded with each other much more frequently than we did with the men above, and some of the goods for which we traded with men were passed on in turn to the Siiri. For they are a very insular people, and refused to venture above the surface to trade."

They waited to hear more, and Ghryzindion continued. "Though my own people preferred to live with each tribe in its own enclave,

113

the Siiri all lived together in one vast underground city near the exact center of the Szariztin range. Nearly a thousand years ago a great sorcerer arose among them, a man who labored long to create ever more intricate spells – with an evil objective. Though the Siiri were not a warlike folk, he gathered around him a society of elite warriors called the Belurii. He equipped them with enchantments to enhance their abilities, and they made him ruler over all of the Siiri people."

Hmm, where was this going? "When the sorcerer, Chtorias, had completed his plans he simultaneously sent bands of his Belurii soldiers – disguised as envoys – to each of the tribes of the Kier Ludzi. They bore gifts for the queen of each tribe, as was appropriate. But as soon as each pomatka laid hands upon the gift, a glowing jeweled orb of great beauty, she was enthralled – linked telepathically to Chtorias and forced to do his bidding."

Adara's mind writhed in revulsion. She had seen close up the effect of sorcerous compulsion, and it was an abomination – the ultimate form of rape. "The pomatkas, one and all, commanded that their people would leave their tribal homes and travel with them, and their escorts of Belurii, to the Siiri city – there to take up the great work of linking all of the underground dwellings of the two peoples into one vast subterranean metropolis. The threat that our pomatkas would be killed should any refuse the order compelled all within the tribes to obey."

"And something happened to the pomatka of the Karindi?" Adara guessed. The old shaman's face took on an expression of great sadness, eyelids drooping.

"There was a faction of younger ones among us, those not two centuries old," he said. "A group of them took up arms and tried to attack the Belurii, hoping to rescue our queen and prevent the relocation and enslavement of our people. Our queen was killed, and when that happened a madness fell up upon the Karindi. The magical enhancements of the Belurii were powerful, and many of our people were killed. But eventually by our greater strength and force of sheer numbers we wiped them out. We sealed the ways leading between our territory and the Siiri city, and went into hiding."

Adara's face was troubled as she asked, "And now only twenty of you remain? Why so few?"

"Some who lived then have since died of old age, such as the master who trained me to become shaman," Ghryzindion replied. "Others have fallen to accident or disease, some have been killed in skirmishes with Belurii. And some have just pined away. Without a pomatka, our tribe is doomed – no longer a tribe, but just a group of individuals waiting to die. The only thing that has kept us alive all this time is the hope that we might somehow find a way to put an end to the Siiri sorcerer and free our people from bondage."

"He has enslaved them?" Adara asked.

"From the day they first arrived in the place the Siiri call Zabran Lokaini, the Kier Ludzi were put to laboring at all the tasks the Siiri preferred not to do. We are far better suited than they for tunneling and mining, and gradually the Siiri abandoned all their labors. They spend their days in artistic pursuits now, while my people live by the sweat of their brows in exchange for rude quarters, enough food to live on, and the knowledge that their tribes will continue while their queens still live."

Those Siiri had better be some damn good artists, Adara thought. "Ghryzindion," she asked, "did your people never consider seeking aid from the men in the world above? You had your trading contacts – might you not have contracted for mercenaries to aid you in your fight, or at least continued trading for the goods that enriched your lives?"

The old one looked down, troubled. "Some argued that we should do so," he admitted. "But always we had met with the humans above, far away from our underground homes. We did not want them coming here, to our heart-place. This is not, you will pardon me, *your* place. And with our numbers so reduced, and our pomatka gone, we had no heart for the making of trade goods. Many argued that we should abandon all contact with the world above, and foremost among those was Inzharion – our shaman. She had assumed the role of leader, now that we had no queen and never would again."

Adara heaved a sigh, for the wickedness that seemed inherent in all sentient beings and the foolishness that seemed to accompany it. "But now we are here," she said. "You did not kill us out of hand for trespassing in what we had thought the long-abandoned place of an extinct people. You have apparently decided to seek outside help at last. Why now, and why us?"

Ghryzindion sat up a little straighter in his stone chair. Adara's none-too-amply-padded rump was already beginning to ache from sitting in hers, but he seemed impervious to discomfort. "Is it not obvious?" he asked. "It is the Darkshield you wear. Over the centuries we have mounted many attempts to reach Chtorias and destroy him, for we theorize that if he were but to die all of his enchantments would die with him."

Adara nodded. "I slew a powerful sorcerer a few months ago," she said. "All he had enthralled with his spells were released at the moment of his death." The old kobold actually grinned at her. "Exactly!" he went on. "It is reasonably easy for us to infiltrate Zabran Lokaini, blending in with the large population of enslaved Kier Ludzi. And though the Belurii are mighty fighters, if taken by surprise they are no match for our greater physical power. But every time we have come within range of striking at the sorcerer himself, his spells drop us in our tracks."

Adara frowned. "But you're a shaman! Have you no magic that would hide you from Chtorias' sight, or shield you and your warriors from his spells?" Ghryzindion hung his head. "It was usual," he said, "that the shaman of the tribe would train his or her apprentice for centuries. The magic of our people, granted by our gods, is complex and far-reaching. Inzharion's apprentice, whom she had guided for more than two hundred years, was among those slain during the madness that erupted when our pomatka was killed. I, as one of the eldest remaining among us, became his replacement. But I had less than a century of training before the mantle, and the staff, fell to me. There is much I do not know."

Now Adara felt like she'd kicked a puppy, which was utterly absurd considering she confronted a being who had been an adult long before the remotest ancestors she could put a name to had been born. "I'm sorry, I didn't know," was all she said. Then, after a pause, "What do you want us to do?" Stellan sat up a little straighter, glad to hear that plural pronoun. The old shaman's demeanor became a little more cheerful, realizing that this remarkable young creature was not arguing – or bargaining – but had apparently just volunteered to help.

He hardly knew where to begin, having expected so much more resistance. The idea of using Adara as a resource had only come to him at the moment when he had seen how she sloughed off his spell of paralysis as if it had not been cast – yet capitulated moments later, when her companions were threatened. In the hours since then his mind had been at work on plans, and he thought he had nearly hammered one out.

"There is a secret way from the home of the Karindi into Zabran Lokaini," he said, "and I know well the way from there to the part of that vast underground city where Chtorias has his private quarters – and the luxurious prison in which the Mothers of the Kier Ludzi reside. It is also the headquarters of the Belurii, but if a small party of us arrives there by stealth during the hours when the Siiri are at rest, it should be possible to slip within. Once Chtorias is dispatched, the Mothers will be free of his compulsion and all of the Kier Ludzi will know it. We are psychically linked with our pomatkas – it is why the madness erupted when the pomatka of the Karindi was killed."

"And then the Kier Ludzi will arise and throw off their chains?" Adara asked, envisioning the colossal upheaval that would result.

"I am sure that would be the case," the old one replied with a slight smile.

"But what of the Belurii? Would there not be slaughter?"

"We are far stronger than the Siiri," he said with a hint of satisfaction as he imagined the outcome. "And armed – with things like picks, shovels, and drills, while the majority of our oppressors are armed with flutes and paintbrushes. The Belurii are only a small force, compared with the might of the entire Kier Ludzi nation. I do not fear them."

Chapter 19

Day and night had no meaning, in the heart-place of the kobolds. For two periods of alertness, and two periods of sleeping – no longer locked in or guarded – Adara and her companions worked to prepare for the assault on Zabran Lokaini: the "Deep Home" of the Siiri.

Though she had fully committed to the task set her and had not tried to negotiate any terms, Adara was determined that there should be some concessions made. "Jaime must remain here in the care of your remaining warriors," she told Ghryzindion. "He is only twelve years of age. But he must be treated with every kindness, not as a prisoner."

The old shaman readily agreed. Should they all perish on this mission, the boy would be set free within easy walking distance of Feingeld, thence to make his way home. She made sure he was amply supplied with gold, so he could hire someone to carry him from Feingeld back to Willoughby. Whatever the outcome of Adara's efforts, her brother would return safely to his family.

There was also the issue of food. Adara and Stellan had not brought all of their food supplies up the mountain for what they had expected to be a short few hours of exploration and perhaps a bit of tomb raiding. Their trail bread supplies were already running low. Despite what seemed like major biological differences, kobolds were still sort-of human. So what had *they* been eating the past seven hundred years, in the absence of trade goods from above?

The answer was surprising. No familiar plants grew in these caverns thousands of feet below the mountains, but that did not mean they were devoid of life. There were fungi that feasted on air and the minerals within rocks, thriving in the glow of blue light from phorium crystals. And on these fungi a host of small animals – most of them blind or nearly so – also fed.

The food was bland in the extreme, but Adara was assured that it would provide enough nutrients to sustain them. What this needs is some Frigan hot sauce, she thought, the first time she sat down to a meat of fungal fruitbodies steamed with the meat of a large arthropod that somewhat resembled a terrestrial crayfish. She had only been separated from the world above for a couple of days, and already she longed for it even more than she longed for Stellan's body.

And that was the third thing. Stellan would accompany her, Ghryzindion, and Brzhandin – the Franca-speaking lieutenant who had once been a fellow trader – on the mission into enemy territory. Adara figured that, even though he was as vulnerable as anyone (besides her) to the Siiri sorcerer's spells, his skills were too valuable to do without. But she doubted they would have any opportunities to get together while they were stealing through the shadows within Zabran Lokaini. She wanted better sleeping accommodations, and she wanted them *now*.

"This complex once housed nearly a thousand people," Ghryzindion told her. "I'm certain we can find some quarters more suitable for you while we gather supplies for our expedition." There were few of the wooden, cloth, and leather goods the kobolds had once traded for still in usable condition. And the kobolds, being a tougher race, had found comfort in conditions a human could scarcely tolerate; but some parts of the Karindi's heart-place were more comfortable than others.

Eventually, they settled on the suite of rooms that had belonged to the last pomatka of the Karindi. These had been sealed off, unused, for most of the past seven hundred years – and while all of the current remnant of the tribe had been alive then and could remember the events surrounding that cataclysm, enough time had passed that they were willing to allow the visitors to stay there.

Jaime ensconced himself in the spacious room that had once been the private quarters of the queen's consort. The king whose tomb they'd invaded had not been the mere consort of a tribal queen, but an overlord of the entire kobold race, in the days long past when the tribes had fought united against foes from the world outside.

The kobold man who impregnated the queen might be someone with whom she had bonded for life, or only a passing fancy. Some queens imported a new consort from neighboring tribes many times during their long reigns, ensuring an enriched gene pool for their descendants.

Jaime was blissfully unaware of all this, though Adara and Stellan had had it explained to them. He only knew that this huge room was three times the size of his room at home, and had a bed with a cunningly-fashioned spring mattress sitting atop the stone platform. The fabric that had once covered it had largely rotted away, but by draping some of his spare clothing and his warm cloak over it, he had a halfway decent bed. Malika had opted to bunk with him. The two had formed a bond, it seemed, and Adara welcomed the situation. The semigryph had discovered underground pools where blind fish swam, and had been eating very well since they arrived.

Adara and Stellan enjoyed a similar bed, ensconced in the very chambers that had once housed the last queen. The first such thing they had slept on, in quite a while. But there were other things to do than sleep, were there not? Bathing was another issue, and they'd had to be content with a quantity of water suitable for washing a meal's worth of pots and pans – heated by Ghryzindion's spells, and used to give each of them a sponge bath. It left them cleaner than they had been since leaving Underhill, and turned out to be enjoyable in its own right.

For the occasion, the shaman had also provided them with a spell that boosted the normal ambient temperature of their quarters to a point where they could get naked without developing goose bumps. The two sat, stripped to the skin, on one of their cloaks that had been spread on the stone floor. Between them, an intricately patterned metal urn contained around four gallons of hot water.

Adara held a bath sponge in her hand, a sea creature pulled from the waters between the continents of Eorla and Frigan at some point in recent history. Gazing into Stellan's eyes, a sweet smile wreathing her features, she dipped it into the urn. Ooh, it was *hot*! She could scarcely imagine anything more delightful. Swiping the wet sponge across the bar of scented soap she'd brought with her from Willoughby, she began by rising to her knees and reaching across to scrub Stellan's neck, shoulders, and upper chest. His cock resembled a small lighthouse.

His dark eyes sparkled in the dim glow. She had decided to treat them to the warm light of one of the torches they'd packed along, though the room was well-supplied with phorium crystals. For those used to daylight, the wan blue light of the crystals left everything looking anemic.

Stellan took the sponge from Adara's hand, dipping it into the hot water and squeezing it out. Then he rubbed it over the bar of soap and repeated her moves, washing her neck and shoulders, skipping over the Darkshield to lave her upper arms – and her breasts. Her nipples stood up as if they were competing with his cock for some sort of erection award.

Eyes dilated to jet black in the torchlight, he dipped the sponge again. "Stand up," he murmured. "I need to wash the rest of you." Adara gazed at him across the top of the urn, an expression of delight on her lovely face, and rose to her feet. He did the same.

Stellan stepped forward and to the side, skirting the still-steaming urn so that they were both standing on the same side of it. He put his left arm around Adara's shoulders, drawing her close to him as he ran the wet, soapy sponge down her belly and around to her back. She sighed gently, her right arm encircling his waist.

They fell into a clinch – mouths locked together, fingers squeezing buttocks as they pressed their bodies tight. Then they broke apart again, and Stellan bent to rinse the sponge once again. He spun Adara around and washed her back, dipping more soap and hot water to wash her buttocks and legs. She was torn – her hunger for cleanliness in a fierce competition with her hunger for Stellan's cock.

Cleanliness won out – for the moment. When she had been washed from head to toe, he passed the sponge back to her. Her eyes were half-hooded, and dilated to the point where they were nearly as dark as his own. Water dribbling down Adara's thigh as she held the sponge at her side, she stepped close to engulf Stellan's mouth in a deep kiss.

His erection had not gone down appreciably since they'd begun this game, but now it swelled still more. It prodded the smooth curve of her belly, hot and insistent. Adara stepped away again, the wet and soap-smeared sponge in her hand, and began rubbing it around Stellan's lower abdomen.

Stellan bit his lower lip, mustering all the control five years of sexual experience had taught him. Adara's touch was like fire, and it took everything he had not to explode as she ran the warm sponge gently around his crotch and then took his throbbing cock into her mouth.

Oh gods, it felt so wonderful! He closed his eyes, suspended on the brink of orgasm, until he thought he could stand it no longer. Then he pushed her away, bringing her back up to her feet, and crushed her in an embrace – his tongue in her mouth, a buttock in each hand.

"Go lie down on the bed while I finish washing," he urged her quietly. She gave him the smallest of smiles, eyes downcast dreamily, and strolled over to their makeshift mattress. She sat on the edge of the bed atop the cloak, watching as Stellan hastily washed his body from the waist down. By now the water was cool enough he could dip his feet into the urn, one after the other.

Clean now, he came to stand before her – member still jutting – and pushed her down gently so that she was lying with her legs hanging over the edge of the bed. Kneeling on a pile of cast-off clothing, he bent his head between her legs and began licking, sucking, probing. A hot, wet rush ran through Adara from her crotch to the top of her head. Ah!

Adara had no need, no desire to postpone orgasm, and the teasing play as they'd washed each other had her already on the brink. Seizing Stellan's head and pressing his face into her crotch as she bucked and cried out, she rode it for an endless moment of ecstasy.

Grinning, Stellan waited until Adara's spasms had subsided. Then he crawled up onto the bed to lie beside her. They lay on their sides face to face, and she threw her leg up over his hip as he guided his eager cock to its goal. "Stellan, oh Stellan," Adara moaned urgently as he moved inside her at last.

The spring mattress was quite noisy, they discovered, especially when subjected to stresses it had likely not known in many centuries. Fortunately, the stone walls of their bedchamber were thick.

Chapter 20

All too soon, the time had run away and their departure for the secret ways into Zabran Lokaini was at hand. In the end, they decided not to bring Malika along with them. "She is silent and stealthy, and I can look through her eyes," Adara pointed out.

"You have the ability to see through the eyes of wild creatures?" Ghryzindion asked.

"Not only wild creatures," she explained. "Any that are not sentient, I can ride and control with my mind." The old kobold's enormous eyes widened still more.

"This power was spoken of, and my old master Inzharion had heard of it but did not know its secrets. It is not part of the magic of our gods."

Adara wondered at these gods of the kobolds. Did they truly exist? Clearly the kobold shaman had spells that worked, and the power must be coming from somewhere. She wasn't even sure that the gods of her own people were anything beyond a nice idea and some entertaining stories. That didn't keep her from praying to Maridem, though, whenever she was in need of divine mercy. And sometimes, those prayers appeared to have been answered.

"In any case, Adara," the old shaman went on, "your little friend is ideally suited by coloring to blend in among forests and rocky peaks. But she would stand out like a beacon within the corridors of the Siiri's underground city." She eyed him questioningly. "The Siiri are truly golden," he explained, "and freed from all everyday labor they have devoted the past centuries to making their environment into a mirror of themselves. The walls within Zabran Lokaini glow golden, pink, or blue, shimmer with crystals, or are decorated with fantastic paintings. To one of my race, the place is an eye-wrenching visual cacophony. But it is in accordance with the artistic tastes of our oppressors."

"And do the Siiri share their underground city with other creatures besides the Kier Ludzi?" Adara asked. "Oh yes," he replied. "Far more plants and animals thrive there than do here, for the Siiri with their arts have molded many living things to live happily belowground." She could hardly wait to see it, though she hoped it would not prove to be the last thing she saw before her untimely death. Infiltrating an alien city where she and Stellan would be the only humans seemed risky in the extreme.

"Very well," Adara told the group. She and Stellan, with Jaime and Malika included, had been discussing their strategy with Ghryzindion and Brzhandin – who would accompany them on their mission. The two kobolds would, they hoped, prevent any kobolds who spotted them from attacking them or raising an alarm. "Jaime, you can keep Malika out of mischief while we're gone. Maybe you can help her practice her flying in the great hall."

Her brother grinned happily. From being devastated when they were captured while exploring the ancient king's tomb, he now felt he was having an exotic adventure with their new friends the kobolds. From time to time it would occur to him that his parents had surely discovered his deceit by now, and that he was going to be in a world of trouble when he got home; but he put it out of his mind. He was even starting to pick up the kobold tongue, trading words with Arzhindin – one of the younger (as in, less than a thousand years old) members of the Karindi who had been learning Franca with an eye to becoming a trader someday before the Siiri's coup had brought her world crashing down.

At last it was time to set off. All four of them were laden with heavy packs, and Adara was clad once again in her irilium plate armor. But the packs born by the humans were scarcely half as heavy as what the kobolds carried. Their race truly was made with the strength of the bones of Q'ur.

They said their goodbyes. Jaime of course was confident that his sister and her (very close) friend would soon be returning in triumph. With any luck, the grateful kobold nation would heap them all with presents in gratitude for their service, and their honor would be so great that Mama and Papa would overlook his infraction.

The eighteen remaining members of the Karindas tribe were cautiously optimistic. All of them had watched their once-mighty tribe dwindle over the centuries; and if their shaman should be lost, his staff would be lost with him. The failure of this mission would mean death for the Karindi, and an eternity in bondage for their Kier Ludzi brethren.

As they approached a heavy metal door at the end of a long, narrow corridor, Ghryzindion explained for the benefit of his human companions, "Here we leave the home of the Karindi behind. This door has been fortified with enchantments by every shaman of our tribe for many thousands of years. Had the Siiri come to us in force – unlikely, since they are ill-suited for war – they could not have passed here though they brought all their sorcerers' spells and a battering ram the thickness of a man to bear. Yet we let them through it willingly, never guessing their treachery."

The door was a foot thick, seemingly made of solid metal, yet so perfectly balanced on its hinges that the old shaman was able, after unlocking it and releasing the enchantments, to push it open with one hand. The corridor beyond it looked identical the one they had passed through for nearly an hour to reach this spot: dark gray stone, occasional clusters of phorium crystals giving off a wan blue light.

Ghryzindion closed the door behind them and renewed the locking spell, assuring no hostile presences could pass through. As he did so, he realized with a sense of aching melancholy that it now protected but eighteen Karindi and one young human boy. What they undertook now had better work. If it did not, he was happy to die in the attempt.

Uncounted hours ran away, as the small party trudged along the corridor. It bent occasionally, presumably in response to changes in the bedrock through which the tunnel had been dug. Adara noticed that there were frequent holes in the ceiling no more than a foot in diameter, probably air shafts. She couldn't detect a breeze, but the air remained fresh and breathable.

Occasionally they would also encounter side tunnels leading off, but they took none of them. "Where do those go?" Adara asked curiously.

"Those tunnels link the underground homes of one Kier Ludzi tribe with another," Ghryzindion explained." "All empty now, or incorporated into the Siiri city. The Karindi heart-place was among the furthest from the original bounds of Zabran Lokaini, which may be one reason why they have not yet reached this point. While my people are the masters of tunneling in rock, even for us it is slow work."

There was no light beyond that from the phorium crystals down here, and no way to measure the passage of time but the exhaustion that slowly crept over Adara and Stellan as they trod the endless corridors. Their strides were longer than those of their kobold companions, but their strength was only human. Finally, after a consultation that mostly consisted of glances and hand squeezes, Adara announced "Ghryzindion, we must rest."

"Very well, then," the old shaman replied. Adara was grateful that there was no suggestion of reluctantly humoring the frail humans, when he (obviously aged) and Brzhandin (a bit younger), both carrying twice the weight, were yet ready to continue for hours.

Adara and Stellan went back down the corridor the way they'd come to relieve themselves, then returned to where the two kobolds had dropped their packs and begun digging out provisions. Even the kobolds had something resembling trail bread, though it was far blander and lacked anything resembling the savor of what the humans had brought with them. Alas, all those supplies were gone now. Eh, it was sustenance.

Though they were physically tired, Adara yet felt that she was not ready to sleep. An hour or so spent making love with Stellan would have sent her off to dreamland happily. As that was not going to happen, she decided to engage their companions in some intimate conversation.

"Ghryzindion, Brzhandin, what was it like for you growing up in your tribe when you were children?" she asked. The question had sent the old shaman into another flood of painful thoughts, but his lieutenant was happy to answer. His command of Franca was not as good, but he was an honest and uncomplicated soul.

"It was wonderful," he replied. "I missed our Mother at first, but everyone was like a mother to me. Or a father, maybe. I don't know. Everyone happy to spend time with me, teach me. In tribes of Kier Ludzi, children rare. We… I think term is 'get away' with everything. Much mischief, much fun."

Adara smiled to herself, trying to imagine this lifestyle so different from that of humans. Every child a special gift, belonging not to its biological parents but to the entire tribe. And though it apparently took a couple of centuries for a child to be considered an adult, that was a small fraction of a lifespan that might be two millennia.

"Did you play with your siblings?" Adara asked, trying to flesh out her mental picture of kobold childhood. "Oh, yes," Brzhandin replied. "We would run everywhere within the home of our people. I think it was the best time. The best time ever…" his voice tailed off. Adara was sorry she'd spoken. To remind these people, whose situation was so dire, of all they had lost was, she realized, no kindness.

"Stellan, how about a song?" she suggested instead. Both their kobold companions had enough Franca to understand simple song lyrics. Whether they had any appreciation of music, she had no idea. But *she* could certainly use a song. He had his cithara out of his pack in an instant, understanding what Adara needed. After tuning the instrument, while the kobolds looked on with interest, he launched into a sprightly melody. Ghryzindion and Brzhandin seemed fascinated.

> *"Well I went to the flowing spring,*
> *Where the water's so good.*
> *And I heard there the cuckoo,*
> *As she called from the wood."*

Likely kobolds had no points of reference for springs, woods, or cuckoos. But their two gray companions were gripped by the purity of the melody, Stellan's fine tenor voice. Adara came in on harmonies, and the look on the kobolds' faces told them that they had just introduced an entirely new experience to these beings who had been living for ages before either of them had been born.

"I have never heard anything like that!" Ghryzindion exclaimed when the last chord had died away. "Do you have more?" The dimly lit, cold stone corridor rang to the sounds as the two humans, infants by the lights of the ancient kobolds, entertained their companions until all were ready to sleep.

Chapter 21

"This door marks the entrance to Zabran Lokaini," Ghryzindion told them in hushed tones." Adara's eyes widened at the sight. They had been traveling for two periods of waking and two of sleeping, and the stone surrounding them was now pale gray. Lighting was still provided by clusters of blue-glowing phorium crystals, but these had begun to be augmented by curious patches, like glass disks, that glowed a pale orange.

The door was much different in appearance from the one that had marked the exit from the home tunnels of the Karindi. For one thing, it appeared to be made of translucent stone. There was no sign of a keyhole. "How do we get inside?" Adara asked. Since the old kobold shaman had told her he had been here many times in the past, it stood to reason there was a way in… but what was it?

He smiled at her. "Why, little one, we but wait for it to be opened to us," he replied. Considering she was nearly four inches taller than he was, the term seemed inaccurate. But considering he was a hundred times her age, perhaps it was apt. Ghryzindion gestured to a doorless opening in the corridor only a few yards away. It was the entrance to a large storeroom, stacked with excavation tools.

"This is the current limit of the Siiri's planned expansion of their city to encompass all of the subterranean workings beneath the Szariztin," the old shaman explained. "Since they rule everything beneath the mountains save the home of the Karindi, they have little to fear. Yet, as the workings carved by my people expand, from time to time these doors are erected as a barrier against intrusion. They are only a formality, and poorly guarded."

Not truly understanding what the old one meant, Adara and Stellan huddled with their kobold companions in the storeroom for close to an hour. They took advantage of the delay to eat from their dwindling stores, and drink from their water skins. He threw an arm over her shoulders, and drew her to him in a deep kiss. A wave of lust came over Adara, though she would have preferred to avoid it. There had been no opportunities for them to get together on this trip through the underground tunnels, and likely would be none until they'd completed their mission or died in the attempt.

Suddenly they heard a creak, and the sound of marching feet. Instantly all four of them were alert, hidden amid the storeroom's contents. A troop of kobold workers came by, bearing hammers, rock drills, picks, and shovels. Accompanying them was the first Siiri either Adara or Stellan had seen.

The figure appeared to be male, unless perhaps the Siiri – like the kobolds – had freemartins among them. Adara doubted it, as the Siiri sorcerer's attack had exploited a biological weakness. If the Siiri had the same weakness, would he have tried such a thing? He stood of a similar height with the gray-skinned laborers, but slender as a rod. His skin was pale golden, seeming to shine with an inner light. He wore only a multicolored robe that looked like it might be made of silk, and a vibrant cascade of finely textured hair in pastel shades hung from the top of his head halfway down his back. His features were finely chiseled, beautiful. In sum, he looked as if someone had taken the standard human form and transformed it into a small, perfect work of art.

Adara stifled a gasp as the rough-hewn kobold workers and their astonishingly lovely escort trooped past. Her human aesthetic sensibilities were warring with her sense of right and wrong. It could be nothing but wrong, to enslave a people by threatening their very existence. But what could be more right, that a race as beautiful as the Siiri should have dominion over their coarse, lumpish cousins?

No, no, no, she told herself. Don't fall into the trap of siding with those you find more visually appealing. While the kobolds' differences from humankind were profound, she had found them to be a people with much to recommend them. And if they themselves were less than elegant, the things they made with gems and metals were as beautiful as the Siiri were themselves.

The troop of workers and their supervisor had left the door open behind them. It appeared that security here was lax. Aside from the Siiri themselves and the kobolds who were forced to submit to bondage while the mothers of their tribes were held hostage, fewer than two dozen individuals in all the thousands of square miles of space beneath the Ratskells even knew this place existed. If the Siiri were less than vigilant, it was no surprise.

Beyond the door, the corridor was double the width it had been. And just as Ghryzindion had said, it was a riot of light and warm color. The corridor's flat, level floor appeared to be made of, or at least tiled with, hard stone. The ceiling was curved, rising to a height of twelve feet at the center and connecting seamlessly with the walls.

Adara and Stellan felt a sense of relief flood over them. Even though the increased visibility here put them more at risk of discovery, the warm light answered a need both of them had felt for the past several days without even realizing it. They were creatures of the world above, the world of sunlight and color; and days spent in the tunnels of the kobolds, in dim blue light, had been oppressive.

They exchanged a glance that told much, then began moving carefully along the corridor behind their kobold guides. There seemed to be nobody in sight, and warm light glowed from various places in the walls and ceiling, and sparkled off of crystalline designs set between the lights. The air was cool and dry, little different from that of the tunnels they'd been traveling through; but the golden light made it *feel* warmer, somehow.

Afraid to speak aloud, Adara closed the gap with Ghryzindion and touched him on the shoulder. He turned to look up at her questioningly, the pupils in his enormous, pale blue eyes contracted to pinpoints. From the standpoint of a creature evolved to live in near darkness, this environment must seem a painful glare. "I would like to search for some of these non-sentient creatures you mentioned, and do some reconnaissance," she told him quietly.

"Good idea," he replied. "Do you need to lie down?"

When Adara had first undertaken to perfect the mind-riding skill Nanny had barely begun to teach her when she'd left home, she had needed to lie down on a bed – seemingly asleep or nearly in a coma. Thanks to her Learning Ring, she was now able to ride the minds of animals while standing up, eyes open, even carrying on a conversation. It was hard, but it was possible.

"Stellan, if you'll just take my arm? I should be all right." He came to stand beside her in an instant, eyes alight with interest. Since Adara's confession of this power to him, the night that Jaime had arrived at exactly the wrong moment, he had not yet seen it demonstrated.

Adara reached out, encompassing a section of the warren that was Zabran Lokaini with her mind. It was not as heavily populated as she had expected. Reaching out still further she found greater concentrations of life forms – mostly the sentient Siiri and their kobold servants – away in a direction she assumed was toward the center of the vast complex. Now, where were the little non-sentient creatures the kobold shaman had mentioned?

Ah, here was a little creature around the size of a rat. But not a rat, Adara realized, as she slipped within its cold, scaly mind and looked out through its eyes. The eyes seemed capable of looking in two completely different directions at once! Its vision provided color information, too – something one could not get from most small mammals, though birds had it.

What… ah, there was another one. The creature Adara was riding was some kind of lizard, it seemed. It was clinging to the walls of the tunnel with sticky pads on its toes, on the lookout for insects to eat. She realized there were quite a few of these creatures, as she jumped from one to another and then checked back to look where she'd been. Their eyes were mounted on swiveling cones, they were covered in fine scales, and they had fairly short, stubby tails.

Encouraging the one she was inhabiting to move on down to the next juncture, Adara took it around a corner for look at what was beyond. A large atrium opened up, with a ceiling more than twice the height of the corridors. The space was circular, with corridors giving off of it like the spokes of a wheel. And in the center, what appeared to be a circular flower bed with plants in it flourished beneath the glow of an artificial orb mounted in the ceiling. Wow!

Clearly the Siiri had seen fit to make living underground a much less gloomy pastime than their cousins the kobolds had done. A great many Siiri seemed to be merely enjoying the space – relaxing on benches, talking with one another. They were all dressed colorfully, and some seemed to be engaged in artistic endeavors. A group of three were working on a mural running around a quarter of the circle defined by the atrium, and several others in the area were watching them. Two in the space appeared to be children, each accompanied by a Siiri man and woman – presumably the child's parents. The women were even more beautiful than the men.

Pulling out of the mind of the lizard-creature, Adara returned her attention to her companions. "There's no one in the immediate area," she said, "but there's a circular open space with a lot of Siiri apparently just relaxing, off in that direction around half a mile from here." Ghryzindion nodded.

"They refer to them as plazas," he said. "As none of them need work at anything they don't enjoy, there are many such spaces where the Siiri can gather to pass the time pleasantly – while my brethren labor at carving tunnels and chambers, growing and preparing food, and so forth." It was plain from his tone what he thought of this situation.

"I notice they all seem to be dressed in silken cloth," Adara remarked. "Do the enslaved Kier Ludzi also make fabrics now?" The old shaman shook his head. "Among the many surface creatures the Siiri have adapted to live underground, there are large worms – larvae of a type of moth – that provide fiber from the cocoons they make. The harvesting, spinning, dying, and weaving of this fiber has always been considered an art form by the Siiri, and clothing is one of the few basic needs of living they still provide for themselves. I think they did not believe that my kind possessed the artistic sensibilities needed for the job."

Zabran Lokaini was a beautiful and fascinating place, but Adara had to keep it in mind that its lovely inhabitants were her enemies. They were not here to be awed by the décor, but to infiltrate the city's heart and murder the Siiri's leader – so that they could free the captive Mothers and restore the enslaved kobolds to freedom. That was going to create a massive upheaval in the Siiri's way of life, but considering they'd lived this way for only seven hundred years – a fraction of an individual Siiri's lifespan – they ought to be able to get over it.

"What do we do now, push on?" Adara asked.

"Better we hide and rest for a few hours, until the night comes," Ghryzindion told her. She looked at him questioningly. "I do not know all the history of the Siiri," he explained, "but it is clear that at one time thousands of years ago they lived above ground. There must have been some terrible, devastating event that caused them to seek shelter belowground. One so awful that they have refused to return to the surface since taking up residence in these caverns beneath the Szariztin. Yet, they fill their underground homes with light and color. And by their arts, they have created a cycle of day and night. A few hours from now, all the lights you see around us will have dimmed to a fraction of their current brightness. And most of the Siiri will be in their chambers, asleep."

Chapter 22

They continued moving in the general direction of what
Ghryzindion said was the exclusive section of the city where
Chtorias had his quarters. He, his mistress, the imprisoned Mothers
of the Kier Ludzi, and the headquarters of the Belurii all resided
there, in an enclave within the greater excavation that was Zabran
Lokaini. Only one well-guarded corridor connected it to the rest of
the city, providing it with security far beyond what they'd seen so
far.

Long before they reached the plaza Adara had seen while riding
the lizard-creature, they turned off down a side corridor and followed
a curving path to an area of the sprawling underground complex that
seemed to be used for the storage and distribution of food. "All of the
city's food is grown on the level below," the old shaman told them
quietly as they made their way stealthily along. "My people have
been conscripted to work the farms, planting and harvesting the
crops and transporting them to distribution points above. As did the
individual tribes of the Kier Ludzi, the Siiri share food communally.
But it's my understanding that Chtorias and the Belurii get more than
their share of the best of it."

The corridor broadened, and at an intersection ahead they turned
to the left. A sign in unfamiliar runes hung above a squared-off
corridor, partially blocked by a stone counter and lacking any of the
ornamentation Adara and Stellan had come to expect. It much more
closely resembled a place of the kobolds, though the light was pale
and warm.

A kobold functionary, dressed in rough-spun clothing apparently
made from some plant fiber similar to hemp, stood behind the
counter. His eyes went wide with shock at the approach of the
intruders. Ghryzindion quickly addressed him (a male, he was sure,
though the difference between males and freemartins when clothed
was subtle) in the language of the Kier Ludzi.

"Be silent, or you will regret it," he said curtly. The clerk
recoiled in horror. He was one of those who'd been born after his
people had gone into bondage, and the sight of this old one wielding
a traditional shaman's staff filled him with horror. Adara and Stellan,

taking this in without any real understanding of what was being said, hung back and remained alert for threats from behind.

"What..." the clerk began, but he was cut off.

"I told you to be silent!" Ghryzindion snapped. "We are here to free the Kier Ludzi by putting an end to the sorcerer Chtorias and releasing the Mothers from bondage. Should you raise any kind of alarm, you will be killed – and likely, the Mother of your tribe will be killed as well. My companions and I will rest here until lightfall, then we will be on our way. You will tell no one that we saw us, and soon you – and all our brethren – will be free."

The clerk gulped. "All right," he said, "but be quick – hide yourselves! The Belurii overseers will be here for the post-mid check before long!" The old shaman turned to Adara and Stellan.

"We will hide here, amid the stores, until the time of darkness has arrived. Hurry, move within!" he commanded, and they obeyed. The cavernous space, lit by many of the orange-glowing circles, stretched on for another hundred feet at least – the area broken up by numerous load-bearing pillars and stacked with metal boxes and fabric sacks of foodstuffs.

The raiding party moved on through the room until they were near the back. With gestures, Ghryzindion directed them to take up hiding places on either side of the central aisle, each of the four finding a niche among the piled goods wherein they could rest for a few hours, waiting for "lightfall" and time to move out again.

Adara gave Stellan a perfunctory kiss, then moved down to the end of the aisle. Metal racks were set at about half the distance from the smooth stone floor to the ceiling, which unlike that in other areas of the complex was flat. She lifted herself up into an open space on the rack's top surface, and took off her pack.

Ugh, she'd have liked to remove her armor as well; but the omnipresent sense of danger was too great. She settled for leaning her back against the pack, legs straight out in front of her, and biting into some of the bland kobold trail rations she had with her. The four of them, each hidden in a niche amid the supplies at the rear of the distribution center, fell into silence. Their unwilling kobold helper would notify them when the Siiri's period of darkness had begun.

In the corridor leading to the distribution center, a pair of Belurii overseers walked their rounds. While the elite Leader's Guard watched over Chtorias and his household within the Leader's Compound, where the Belurii also had their headquarters, the vast majority of those Siiri who'd chosen combat as their preferred art form did duty as overseers.

They patrolled a beat in pairs, keeping the peace and ensuring that the Leader's rules were obeyed. And more importantly, they kept an eye on the subjected kobolds to ensure that they were fulfilling their assigned tasks and were not engaged in sabotage or plotting revolution.

The threat that a tribe's pomatka would be killed should any fail to serve faithfully had never been carried out, though individual kobolds had sometimes kicked over the traces in the centuries since Chtorias' coup had been launched. The Siiri feared, and rightfully so, that to kill one of the kobold Mothers, who were psychically linked with their tribe members, might precipitate a murderous rampage that would cost many lives.

Instead, it was thought better to keep a tight rein on the kobold workers, stamping out any resistance as it was encountered and punishing those involved with a swift and unpleasant death. So far, the system seemed to be working. The two overseers, resplendent in their iridium armor that had been treated to scintillate in rainbow colors as they moved, approached the desk manned by Przhirion, the kobold clerk whose cooperation Ghryzindion had coerced.

They spoke in the Siiri tongue, more closely related to the language of the pinudur than to that of the kobolds. Though some of the Siiri had learned the kobold tongue of old, when the two peoples had been trading partners, as overlords they insisted that all must learn to speak like civilized people. The kobold tongue was harsh and unpleasant, to their finely attuned ears.

"Let me see the ledger," Siurias demanded in a tone that brooked no argument. He and his partner Liumas had been here at the beginning of the work day, establishing a baseline for the expected ledger entries. Belurii command thought it likely that one of the ways in which the kobold servants might seek to work against their masters was in the production, storage, and distribution of the food that was grown on the level below.

The clerks in charge of this network must needs be brighter than their fellows who labored in tunneling and mining, which made them still more suspect. Might they be siphoning off more food for the kobolds, or taking bribes from Siiri citizens to funnel the choicest foodstuffs to them – when all such were reserved for Leader Chtorias and the elite Belurii?

Przhirion felt icy fingers climbing up his spine, though the pair of overseers always came here at this hour of the work day. They had checked his ledgers and the storeroom itself thrice daily for as long as he'd held this position; but never before had he been hiding free kobolds and some bizarre tall creatures he guessed were humans from the world above, tucked in among the foodstuffs at the back of the warehouse. Drops of perspiration formed on his bald pate, running down into his eyes.

His panic rose, as he realized that the perspiration was a dead giveaway that something was wrong. He hastily swiped an arm across his forehead, and Siurias looked up from his perusal of the entries – goods received, goods released – to pierce the kobold clerk with his dazzling rainbow gaze. "What is the matter, Przhirion?" he asked sharply.

"N-nothing, overseer!" the kobold snapped, trying and failing to get a grip on his fear. He had never known what it was like to be free, never lived as a true member of the Kier Ludzi; and the realization of the likely consequences for discovery of what he'd done was terrifying.

Seeing the usually placid clerk, one he'd always judged too timid to try anything, in a state of obvious anxiety, caused the Belurii sergeant to sharpen his scrutiny still more. Something was amiss here, and he meant to get to the bottom of it. "Liumas, take a little walk around the storehouse please," he commanded his corporal.

Przhirion's complexion, normally a light gray, went the color of thick ice – huge eyes widening to the point where the whites were showing around the pale blue irises. "Please, sir, there was nothing I could do!" he stammered. "They just came in and threatened to kill me!"

Siurias drew his gleaming irilium sword with his right hand, his left holding his rod of office. The foot-long, inch-thick metal rod might have been used for a truncheon, but it had another purpose. Enchanted by Leader Chtorias especially for the use of the Belurii patrols, it would paralyze its target for a period of five minutes – ample time in which to use other means to subdue a lawbreaker. Though the modern Belurii had been founded as an elite warrior society, in imitation of the mighty soldiers of millennia ago when the Siiri had lived aboveground and fought many enemies, they had not actually had to kill anyone in hundreds of years.

"They?" the overseer sergeant asked sharply, and the cowering clerk gestured toward the rear of the storehouse. He seemed to be on the verge of curling up in a hysterical ball, and Siurias dismissed him with a gesture. He motioned to Liumas to flank him as he set off down the central aisle, all senses alert.

Gods-damned coward, Ghryzindion snarled to himself. He'd heard the entire exchange, and knew that trouble was coming for them. Alone of their party, he had a good command of the Siiri tongue. This had to be one of those Belurii patrols he had seen but never confronted. They had functioned as Zabran Lokaini's police force in the centuries between Chtorias' rise to power and the coup that had destroyed the Karindi, and as a trader he had visited here several times yearly.

The Belurii were formidable, he knew – but so were he and his companions. And they outnumbered the patrol two to one. All four intruders were alert now, slipping quietly from their hiding places. The shaman told them with hand-gestures, "Be ready – I am going to attack them first." Staff in hand, paralysis spell in readiness, he stepped suddenly out into the aisle.

"There!" Siurias cried out, just as his partner brought his rod to bear and the old kobold collapsed to the floor not two paces from the rear wall. The staff he was holding fell from his lifeless fingers. The two Belurii eyed each other questioningly. An old kobold shaman, here?

Przhirion had said there was more than one intruder, but where were the rest? He or they must be lurking in that last corridor at the rear of the space. Brandishing his sword, Siurias stalked silently forward. He shoved the motionless kobold out of the way with the toe of his boot, pushing the staff further out of reach. Liumas trailed him slightly, rod at the ready.

Brzhandin, Stellan, and Adara did not know what had befallen Ghryzindion, but from the lack of his reporting success, they assumed something had gone wrong. They stayed hidden. Let their antagonists come to them, where they could attack them from both sides of the aisle at once!

Siurias was concentrating his attention on the corridor to the left side of the central aisle, as it was from there the old kobold had appeared. Brzhandin had retreated slightly down the corridor, and as the Belurii sergeant spotted the well-armed kobold and fired at him with his rod, Stellan stepped out into the corridor, sword swinging, to take him from behind. He dropped to the floor with a clatter as Liumas used his own rod on the strange-looking intruder.

Shit, Adara thought, as she realized the odds had just gone from 4-2 in their favor to 2-1 against. She was fairly confident that those rods were not lethal – some kind of paralysis spell, she guessed, such as Ghryzindion himself had used on Stellan and Jaime. She hoped it was one that would wear off by itself!

The second of the Siiri guards (and surely, these must be the fabled Belurii she'd been told about?) had joined his companion in the rear corridor and was staring at Adara. She overtopped him by three inches, and clad in gleaming iridium plate looked like nothing he had ever seen before. While he gaped she made ready to bring Voleur to bear. "Hit him!" Siurias commanded, and the two pointed their rods at the menacing figure and activated the spells. Nothing happened.

Beneath her armor and padding, Adara felt the Darkshield pulse with warmth. She grinned evilly and advanced on them, blade swinging. All members of the Belurii were required to spend a few hours a week at sword practice, but their lack of anyone to actually *use* those swords on had robbed their training of its edge. Neither had Adara ever turned Voleur on a living foe in earnest; but the skill she'd acquired with the help of her Learning Ring was beyond anything taught in the depths of Zabran Lokaini.

The overseers were hampered by trying to fight side-by-side in the close quarters of the narrow corridor, and put off-balance by the utter strangeness of their foe and the mystery of the rods' failure to drop him (for they failed to recognize Adara as female) as they had done for the other three.

Adara brought her blade, inches longer than those of her opponents, up and over in a complex maneuver that slid past Liumas' guard and slashed him across the face. The bastard-sword's razor-sharp, double-edged tip cut deep across the Siiri warrior's cheeks, eyes, and the bridge of his nose – at a depth of two inches, penetrating through the delicate facial bones and piercing his skull. He fell dying, tangling his sergeant's feet as he went down.

Her opponents were well-armored from head to toe in irilium, as strong and protective as her own, and it was hard for Adara to find an opening. She'd brought down the man she judged to be the junior officer with a lightning, unexpected maneuver – a lucky shot. Even with her several inches of extra reach, hitting the remaining man in a place where Voleur (good quality steel, but only steel nonetheless) could penetrate was difficult. She advanced, blade dancing like a live thing, pushing him steadily back.

Siurias was in shock. What manner of creature was this? It was as tall and graceful as any of the pinudur, the race of elves Siiri legend claimed once lived side by side with them in the lands above before the coming of men. And how had it resisted the rod? If it were a sorcerer, why fight with swords? All these thoughts crowding his mind put him at a disadvantage, and when he reached the central corridor he backed down it. At the far end of that corridor Przhirion cowered, terrified at what he had done.

He had betrayed a shaman of his own race, one whose goal was to free the Kier Ludzi from bondage! Having lived his entire life without knowing any other way, the bondage of his people had seemed the norm – safe, known, unchanging. It was not only the fear of the personal repercussions should the Siiri masters learn he had harbored insurgents that had led to his alerting the overseers. He feared, too, the loss of what to him seemed a comfortable, a reasonable, lifestyle.

But now one of the overseers had failed to reappear in the corridor, and the other was hard-pressed by that tall, iridium-armored warrior! He had no doubt that should the shaman awaken from his rod-induced paralysis while the battle still raged, his own death would be swift and painful – just as the shaman had promised. He must do something!

The contents of the store room were mostly foodstuffs in boxes and sacks, the latter made from the same woven cloth as the clothing provided to the kobold workers. Nothing resembling a weapon, such as miners and excavators had access to. But like all of his race, Przhirion was immensely strong. He seized a nearby fifty-pound sack of tubers, part of a consignment that had recently been delivered, and began working his way through the aisles – trying to circle around the retreating overseer so he could use the heavy sack as a weapon against the tall warrior.

Adara had a clear view of the clerk as he picked up his makeshift cosh, and knew immediately he did not intend to use it against her opponent. For whatever reasons, it was clear he had alerted the authorities to their presence. But why had only two arrived? She would have thought that many more would come. She had not understood any of the recent conversations.

The kobold clerk clambered across the tops of some crates that were stacked along an aisle near the part of the central corridor where Adara and the Belurii officer sparred. From the way he was swinging that sack, he meant either to use it as a bludgeon or perhaps as a missile – aimed at distracting her so her opponent could get past her defenses.

She eased off a little, letting the Belurii push her back somewhat toward the rear of the room and a little further away from where the clerk stood atop his box. Then she leapt nimbly atop a box in the next aisle, and from that to one stacked two high in the aisle where the clerk was perched. He stared at her, aghast.

Siurias was taken aback at his opponent's sudden retreat. Did this strange warrior mean to escape, leaving his companions behind? Leery of climbing up while his enemy held the higher ground, he stood at bay with his sword held upright, ready to respond to the next move.

Adara's next move was to leap across the aisle onto the box next to the one on which the kobold clerk stood. He reacted by swinging the lumpy sack at her head. She bent at the waist, dodging the blow, and then came up with a sweep of the sword that cut a deep gash in the kobold's midsection before slashing the sack open. She ducked again, cringing, as the air was suddenly filled with a rain of hard, roughly spherical objects about the size of her fist.

The kobold clerk fell back with a cry, blood no different in appearance from that of any human's gushing from his wound, and slipped off of the box to the floor of the aisle beyond. The Belurii warrior, taken utterly by surprise, lost his footing as he trod on a rolling tuber and leaned forward, struggling to maintain his balance. Instantly Adara slashed down again, taking him in the back of the neck where it was exposed and severing his spine.

Chapter 23

It was only another minute or so before first Ghryzindion, then the other members of the raiding party who'd been felled by the overseers' rods, regained their power of movement. Adara was exceedingly glad. For all she'd known, the paralysis caused by the rods was something that could only be removed by another spell. She had hastily dragged the body of the warrior she'd killed back to the rear and a short way down the aisle so he was not visible from the entrance. There was rather a lot of blood splashed around, but most of it was in the side aisle where the kobold clerk lay dying.

As soon as he was on his feet again, the old shaman took charge. He surveyed the bodies of the two Belurii, shaking his head in wonder. "A regular patrol," he explained, which sent another wash of relief through Adara. She'd been sure that they'd be up to their armpits in these heavily-armored warriors in minutes at best. "I am quite impressed, young Adara, that you were able to defeat them. The Belurii are acknowledged as among the best-equipped and most highly-trained warriors in Eorla – above or below ground."

She nodded in appreciation of his compliment. "A team bringing more produce from the farms or a requisition for food disbursement may arrive at any time," Ghryzindion went on. The system had not changed significantly since his first visit to the city of the Siiri a thousand years before – only the personnel. "We must hide the bodies."

Brzhandin and Stellan took corpse of the kobold clerk to the rear aisle where the bodies of the two Belurii patrolmen already lay, while Adara picked up and disposed of the rolling tubers and the shaman used his magic to remove all traces of the blood that had been spilled. "The blood of one's enemies is a traditional offering to our gods," he told her casually. Some gods, Adara thought. But as long as it worked...

They got the three bodies tucked in among the boxes of non-perishable foodstuffs on the upper shelf of the rack in the rear aisle. They were invisible to anyone standing on the floor, but the corpses would soon enough begin to stink. "As soon as the next group comes here to collect or deposit food, the clerk's absence is going to cause alarm," the old shaman warned. "We need to be on our way, and find someplace else in which to wait until lightfall."

They plundered some of the containers, making off with enough food to carry them for several days. By then, they expected, they would either be successful in their mission – or dead. By the greatest of good fortune, no one came during the time they were making their preparations to leave. Soon they were stealing off again, taking side corridors whenever they encountered them with an aim to find areas of Zabran Lokaini that were less-densely populated.

The four companions spoke little as they made their way along. As the two kobolds and Stellan kept their senses alert, Adara's mind ranged out ahead of them – sensing life forms in their area. While the area she searched with her mind rendered each living thing as a pinpoint of light, it did not show the corridors that made up the sprawling warren of the Siiri city. She could only extrapolate by the path they tread whether the life she sensed ahead of them was something they were likely to encounter, sharing this particular corridor.

Stellan walked beside her with a hand on her elbow, whenever she quested outward. Though she could to some extent split her attention between the life surrounding them and her own body, it was difficult enough that his help was welcome. After more than an hour of traveling thus, expecting enemies to descend on them at any moment, they found a somewhat narrower corridor and turned down it.

"We are in one of the older parts of Zabran Lokaini," Ghryzindion told them. "Though the addition of the entire Kier Ludzi nation to the city's population severely impacted the availability of living space following Chtorias' coup, I believe that my people's efforts at tunneling over the past centuries have led to an expansion away from the core. This corridor looks nearly deserted, does it not?"

The walls glowed yellow, orange, and rose; but the designs seemed outdated somehow – not in keeping with what Adara had seen, for instance, in the plaza she'd glimpsed through the eyes of the lizard creature. And there was a slight layer of dust on the floor!

"Ghryzindion, can you do anything about our footprints?" she asked. The old shaman shook his head. "I have no spell for that," he admitted. Blood he could always get rid of – dust was another story. "I think I can help," Adara said, and called Ariel. A breeze arose out of nowhere, sweeping dust from ahead of them back down the corridor to cover their tracks.

"How did you do that?" the old shaman demanded. That there were other entities besides the gods of his people to call on had not really occurred to him. Adara hedged. Though she felt they were friends, she didn't want to reveal all her secrets. "It's a power I have," she answered shortly. "I can call air, fire, water or earth to my needs."

Ghryzindion recalled the gout of flame that had swept through the Karindi at the time they'd captured the intruders. How fortunate he and his people were not particularly flammable! They continued down the corridor, and came to a nondescript stone door. "Allow me," Stellan said – putting himself forward for almost the first time since they'd embarked on this quest.

He pulled a set of lockpicks from a pouch at his waist and set to work on the lock. Seemingly the state of the locksmith's art in this ancient elven city was far below modern standards; yet the metals they had used, however many thousand years ago, had not corroded. In less than a minute there was a loud click, and the door swung open.

Adara didn't ask him how he had acquired such skill. It was a discipline she had intentionally not yet mastered, as she had no intentions of becoming a thief. The red Swinzen gold taken from the Bloodspire she didn't see as stolen, really – at least not by her. It had been stolen from some mine in another universe, perhaps. But she and Ferdyn had merely salvaged it after neither those to whom it had once belonged or he who had taken it from them were in a position to reclaim it.

The chamber that opened to them had probably once been a storeroom of some kind. It might have held supplies or equipment, something seldom needed but valuable enough to warrant a lock on the door. The Siiri, despite their communal economy, were no more immune than any other humanoids to the impulse to seek individual advantage.

What it held now was dust and cobwebs. There were a couple of small holes in the ceiling, providing ventilation, and through these no doubt subterranean spiders had come seeking a quiet place to lie in wait for their tiny prey. At least there was air to breath, and light to see by. Only a couple of the orange-glowing discs had been set into the walls of this small chamber – around fifteen by twenty feet in size. But they were enough.

Stellan used his picks to lock the door again from the inside, and Adara asked Ariel to sweep the entire corridor from one end to the other. Should any come seeking them, this corridor would offer no evidence of their passage. In terms of when they'd awakened from their last sleep, it was still early afternoon – and she was not sleepy. But if they were to begin moving by "night," they were all going to need some rest.

"This chamber should go black when lightfall comes," Ghryzindion told them. "These phorium crystals will supply enough light for us to find our way out again." He laid out a handful of the blue-glowing crystals near the door. "Let us all now get some rest, until it is time to move again."

Chapter 24

The kobolds remained awake, but to Adara's surprise she actually managed to doze off for a while. She hoped it would help. Stellan had lain down beside her, his strong arm wrapped around her body, and something about that situation had triggered a sensation of safety that had let her drift off. When she awakened, she wondered at it. She and Stellan were partners, equals – though technically on this expedition she was supposed to be his boss. What was it about being in his arms, that told her subconscious mind it was safe to relax? It had been her, not him, who had defeated their recent foes.

What had brought her to consciousness was Ghryzindion's announcement, "Lightfall has come. Let us be on our way." She quickly got to her feet, but realized that she was hungry again. She had eaten nothing since those few bites of trail rations when they had first hidden in the storeroom.

"Perhaps we should have something to eat first?" Adara suggested. Once again she got the feeling that frail, short-lived humans could only be regarded as children by the Kier Ludzi. But if so, might they not be inclined to protectiveness? They were.

"Good idea, Adara," Ghryzindion said. "Let us all eat and drink before we resume our journey toward the Leader's compound. It will likely be many more hours before we reach it – and I know not what the situation may be along the way. It was my mistake to try forcing that clerk to hide us, when we had better sought quarters such as these."

Adara was astonished. In her experience with leaders, which admittedly was limited, there were few who would so openly admit their shortcomings. The old shaman had misjudged the clerk, assuming that he would automatically side with them just because he was kobold. But it occurred to her that the twenty-nine remaining kobold Mothers must have birthed thousands of children in the centuries since Chtorias' coup. And more than two-thirds of those children would now be adults, having never known what it was like to live in traditional Kier Ludzi society. Now wonder they'd been betrayed!

147

Feeling a sense of satisfaction, Adara sat back down and dug into her pack (which she could barely see, in the light from the cluster of phorium crystals near the door) to find a sack of a grainy substance. It was something they'd liberated from the storeroom, and she decided to go ahead and try it. Mmm, it was crunchy and slightly sweet, with a hint of a nutty flavor to it. How in the world had such a substance been produced here, thousands of feet beneath the surface of the Ratskells?

"Try this, Stellan," Adara urged, and held out a handful. It was a little dry, but their water skins were full. I wonder where the Siiri's alcohol is stored, Adara thought idly as she munched away. She had yet to encounter any humanoids with access to carbohydrates, who had not figured out how to produce alcoholic beverages. The two humans ate their snack, taking frequent pulls from the water skins, while their kobold companions did the same. In the near darkness, Stellan put a hand on her knee and ran it up her thigh. "I want you," he murmured in her ear.

A warm thrill shot through Adara at his words. It was so insane! Here they were, crouched in a dark dusty stone cubicle in the bowels of the earth, with a couple of elderly kobolds for company – in the midst of a desperate mission to fight their way past a nearly unstoppable force, to slay a powerful sorcerer and free a people in whom neither of them had any vested interest. And all either of them could think about, it seemed, was sex!

"It's going to have to wait, love," Adara murmured back. She hoped those huge kobold ears weren't picking up their every word. She ran her own hand up his leather-clad thigh, and squeezed the bulge she found at his crotch. He expelled a breath, but said nothing in reply.

They soon headed out, to find the deserted corridor outside the storeroom in near darkness. Ghryzindion handed Adara a small rod, on the tip of which was set a single large phorium crystal. It cast a circle of dim blue light wide enough that she could see where to place her feet – not that there was much to trip over, here within Zabran Lokaini. By whatever arts they possessed, the Siiri had carved floors that were utterly flat and smooth from the bedrock beneath the mountains.

All of them were alert for danger. By now, someone would have come to the food transfer station – either delivering or requesting a consignment – and found nobody home. Whether or not they had then managed to discover three bodies hidden on the top shelf at the rear, an alarm would have been raised. While the majority of the citizens were normally asleep in their beds at this hour, it was likely that many more of the Belurii would be out and about – actively hunting for the missing personnel or for intruders.

Though Ghryzindion was the leader of their expedition, Adara now found herself the one deciding where they went and when. At each turning he explained to her the direction in which they needed to go, but it was her remote vision, obtained from Zabran Lokaini's "night shift" of vermin, that decided what path they would use to get there.

The lizards had all somehow vanished, finding crevices in which to spend the "night." And out of other crevices had come little mammals, likely nothing the Siiri had intended should share their underground hideaway. They scurried along corridors looking for anything edible, drinking from the occasional fountains. It was at those same fountains that the party of intruders were able to refill their water skins.

As near as Adara could tell, the creature she rode was midway in size between a mouse and a rat. She caught glimpses of other scurrying forms, but unless she could bring her current host up before a mirror she had only a guess as to its identity. Whatever it was, it encountered far more Siiri than was usually the case at this hour – or so she assumed.

Ghryzindion had explained to her that the majority of the Belurii acted as a police force for the city, patrolling in groups of two like those she'd killed. That pattern held, but where normally during the time of relative darkness (only one glowing disk in five remaining lit, throughout the many corridors) there would have been far fewer patrols, it appeared that the Belurii presence had been doubled or tripled. Furthermore, it was clear that they were on the lookout for something specific. Not a single patrol paid the creature she was riding the slightest bit of attention, though it was not – as were the lizards – a desired part of the life of the city.

Adara was soon feeling exhausted. Not only did she have to maintain enough awareness of her body, even with Stellan's solicitous help, to put one foot in front of another; she must constantly be aware of her "mount's" position relative to their party. The tiny legs of the rats and mice or whatever they were could not begin to keep pace with a party of humanoids, so she must frequently jump from one host to another.

Time and again she broke from her contact to warn her companions, "Patrol up ahead." They would have to find a side corridor ahead to go down, or retreat some distance until one could be found – all the while trying to maintain an awareness of where they were, and where they were trying to go. Maridem, what an ordeal!

The labyrinthine nature of Zabran Lokaini finally did them in. Adara had acquired another of the rat-creatures some dozens of yards ahead and was taking it along a corridor Ghryzindion had said led in the direction they must go, when suddenly a pair of Belurii patrolmen emerged from a side corridor and confronted them in shock.

"Halt, show your identification!" the senior of them demanded. That was his mistake, born of centuries when there had been no real threats to confront. Ghryzindion raised his staff, and before the senior patrolman or his associate could draw their rods both of them had collapsed to the floor of the side corridor – paralyzed.

Adara had severed her connection with the little creature she'd been riding to pay attention to the present threat. The chance she'd be called upon to defeat another pair of the heavily-armored Belurii alone was foremost in her mind. Damn, how she wished she could just duplicate the Darkshield a few times to protect her entire party! Or that she knew some real magic, a spell that might have the same effect.

The four of them stood in a circle, looking down at the immobile guardsmen. "What now?" Adara asked, dreading the answer. Ghryzindion shook his head. It was not the way of the Kier Ludzi to kill a helpless opponent. But these two could not be allowed to spread the word that the intruders they sought had been spotted.

"Brzhandin, assist me," he said in their own language. While Adara and Stellan watched in fascinated horror the two old kobolds bent to their fallen foes. It required little of the fabled kobold strength to snap the necks of the relatively gracile Siiri warriors. Adara turned her head away, conflicting emotions swirling inside. Their foes were so attractive, so seemingly worthy of admiration! But giving in to that feeling would no doubt lead to all their deaths, and centuries more of bondage for the Kier Ludzi.

The two kobolds hoisted the dead Belurii up onto their shoulders with little effort, and went seeking down the corridor they'd been traveling along for a hiding place. This was one of the wider thoroughfares, leading in the direction of the Leader's Compound. But many smaller ways gave off of it.

Shaken by her failure to spot the danger coming in from their left, Adara reached out again. She had become too focused on her rat's-eye view, and had not remembered that she had the ability to see *all* the living things in the area – their positions, their movements, and their nature – all without needing to look out through the eyes of any of them. She'd been doing it wrong!

They all hesitated for a few moments, Stellan keeping a tight grip on Adara's arm, as she assessed all the life forms within two miles of their current position. Drawing back, she spoke. "The nearest patrol is up the corridor we're in, I think, and moving in the same direction we are. Everything else in the area is non-sentient. But there seems to be a narrow corridor up a few hundred yards to our left – and there are no sentients along it."

Her ability could detect sentient beings whether they were awake or asleep, a valuable asset for them as most of the Siiri city slumbered. They turned up the next corridor and soon encountered a door on the left. "Nothing bigger than an insect is inside," Adara told them, and in short order Stellan had opened the lock.

The limp bodies of the two Belurii patrolmen were deposited in a storeroom that contained an assortment of cast-off furniture. Stellan had already availed himself of what pieces of armor and weaponry might serve him from the bodies of the two Adara had killed at the food transfer station, and they left these two unplundered. Adara felt a pang, imagining that their victims had left behind loved ones. For beings with lives so much longer than those of humans, might not the loss of those lives be infinitely more tragic? She couldn't say.

They'd been moving for hours, and Adara wasn't sure she could keep this up much longer. Trying to keep her mind in two places at once was beginning to wear her down, and the emotional strain of killing had taken its toll as well. She needed food, she needed rest, she needed to pee.

"Ghryzindion, how much further do you think it is to the Leader's Compound?" Adara asked. He had explained that the Kier Ludzi, supposedly designed by their creators for a life underground, had an inborn sense of direction and an awareness of their own position relative to known landmarks. It seemed impossible, but so far he had not led them wrong.

"We are not that far," he replied. "But we can expect that the number of patrols will only increase as we draw closer. I deeply regret that my error led to our enemies' becoming alerted to our presence." Adara took this in. They didn't need their leader getting cold feet, or doubting his own abilities.

"It was a mistake anyone could have made," she replied. "We just have to deal with it. But I think it would be a good idea if we holed up for a few hours. If the patrols find no one, their vigilance may waver. They'll start convincing themselves that all the excitement was for nothing. After all, how many centuries has it been since they've had a real threat to deal with?"

"Not as many as you might think, young hu-man," the old kobold replied with a hint of wry regret. "We have tried many times to penetrate their defenses over the years. It is why there are so few of the Karindi remaining." Adara had to remind herself yet again that a human's perspective on time seemed absurdly limited to the udur, whose lifespans were more than twenty times her own.

"Even so," she said, trying hard to ignore the old shaman's implication that the mission they were on had a woefully low success rate. "Rest and food would do us all some good. What else lies down this corridor, do you suppose? I sense no life forms at all, at least none bigger than an insect."

They tried the next door down, finding another small storeroom. This one was mostly full of metal trunks, containing who-knew-what. But the one after that opened on an apparently unused apartment. There were no more than one or two small vermin here, which suggested the place was not regularly occupied. Humans, and their long-lived cousins, provided plentiful surplus to support a horde of hangers-on when they were in residence.

"No one has lived here in some time," Adara reported, as they stepped hesitantly inside. The day-night cycle within the Siiri city evidently worked everywhere – corridors, public spaces, and private residences – by turning down the light output of the embedded glowing elements in the walls and ceilings by a factor of 95%. Some areas had more of these elements, others less. In here, there was still just enough light for Adara and Stellan to see by.

They began exploring. Adara guessed that unless the Siiri liked living with roommates, most of their dwellings would be pretty small – since a married couple would only have one child. It occurred to her that she really had no idea how most of the udur lived. Was lifetime marriage even a thing, given you might have 1800 years until "when life is done" – as the traditional Tanar wedding ceremony put it?

The apartment was indeed small, but luxurious by the standards of most Tanar citizens. Ferdyn's Carlienne townhouse, located a few blocks from the royal palace, was much larger and more opulent. But few other places Adara had ever spent time in were so beautifully decorated or well-supplied with amenities. And she guessed that whatever other work the enslaved kobolds were put to, the Siiri did not use them for household servants. Likely the aurudur's lumpish gray cousins were considered too unaesthetic.

There was a good-sized living area, devoid of furniture though there were silken, deep-pile carpets covering the stone floor. Off of that, behind a closed door, was a bedroom – again with carpets, and no furniture except a double bed. It lacked sheets, but the mattress looked like the most comfortable thing the humans had slept on in days. Adara immediately claimed the room for herself and Stellan, a little frisson of anticipation chasing away some of the emotional funk that had come over her after they'd killed those patrolmen.

There was also an area with built-in cabinets and counters, which was probably intended for food storage and consumption, and

– wonder of wonders – a good-sized bathroom with a sunken tub and a hole in the floor apparently intended for wastes. But where was the source of water? Ghryzindion smiled when he saw this facility. They'd been relieving themselves in random corners since the expedition began, leaving evidence of their passage for any to see – and smell.

"I have to admit," he told the humans, "the Siiri have developed their living quarters to a much greater extent than have the Kier Ludzi." He gestured to the hole in the floor. "You deposit your wastes here, then press this knob." There was a whooshing sound, and jets of water squirted down from around the circumference of the hole. "The wastes are all carried to the level below, where they are composted to serve as fertilizer for the farms that provide all of the food for Zabran Lokaini."

Adara and Stellan were fascinated. She turned to the tub, which had a hole in the bottom of it covered by a metal stopper. There were two knobs similar to the one for the waste hole on the wall at one end of the carved stone tub, and a handsome metal spigot protruded from between them. Could it be...?

It was! By what Adara could only imagine was a completely different mechanism, this apartment's bathroom was supplied with hot and cold running water just as the private baths on the ground floor of the Willoughby Hotel had been. Her mood was improving by the moment, and she started the tub filling with a mix of hot and cold water before announcing, "I'm going to have a bath. Stellan, will you join me?"

There was the faintest hint of a grin playing around his lips as he nodded slightly, glancing at their kobold companions. Ghryzindion and his lieutenant exchanged a glance that seemed to say, "What can you expect from a pomatka and her consort?"

Chapter 25

The day's activities had been exhausting, both physically and psychically. But as Adara peeled off her armor for the first time in three sleeps and wrapped herself in the towel she'd optimistically brought along in her pack, she felt a great weight lifting from her shoulders.

Tomorrow night they would infiltrate the Leader's Compound, kill Chtorias, and free the Kier Ludzi Mothers from their long captivity. The details of how they were to achieve all this were something she had not yet worked out. But there was time in which to plan. And for now, she was about to have a hot bath with the man whose presence send her tingling from head to toe – radiating from the crotch.

Stellan, too, had brought a towel. The two made their way from the bedroom where they'd left their packs and armor across the hall to the bathroom and closed the door. Their kobold companions were relaxing in the apartment's living area.

They hung their towels on some elegant-looking metal hooks that were fastened to the dazzlingly patterned stone wall. Almost every stone surface they'd seen since arriving in Zabran Lokaini had artwork on it – paint, tiles, or something that resembled gem-infused stucco. The Siiri didn't go in for representational art, it seemed. No portraits, landscapes, or still-lifes were to be seen, nor had they seen any sculptures. Swirling abstract patterns surrounded the occasional glowing light disks, or glowed with their own light.

Adara and Stellan stood facing one another beside the tub, which was set into the floor and was lined with smoothly polished, gold-veined marble. It was almost too pretty to dirty up by climbing inside it, but the hot water beckoned. Unsurprisingly, his cock was standing at attention. She eyed it appreciatively, but kept her hands off for the moment. First, they would get clean!

The water had been too hot coming out of the tap but had cooled in the time it took for them to undress. Now it was perfect! Adara stepped down into the tub, which was three feet deep by three feet wide and nearly seven feet long. Aahhhh! Now that they were alone,

Stellan gave a full toothy grin at her reaction. Then he stepped in and seated himself at the opposite end.

Adara had brought along the sponge, and her bar of soap as well. They sat soaking for a while, just drinking in the wonderfully relaxing heat. Then she submerged herself and came up dripping, an impish grin on her face. She soaped her hair, rinsed it, then used the sponge to begin scrubbing herself from the neck down. She handed the soap to Stellan so he could wash his own hair, which was lank from days without a shampoo.

He'd always stayed clean-shaven for as long as she'd known him, but there'd been few opportunities to shave since this trip had begun. He now had a several-days' growth of nearly black beard and moustache, which made him look piratical. Adara wasn't sure whether she liked it. He was a devastatingly handsome young man, either way. Nor had their days of intimacy done away with his air of mystery. She still felt there were many secrets he had not shared – and perhaps never would.

Adara twisted herself around until she was facing away from him. "Time to do my back," she said. Stellan's eyes lit as he hastily scrubbed his own front side before scooting closer to her. He sat with his knees bent, legs straddling her body from behind, as he scrubbed her from the nape of the neck down to her buttocks. He cupped some water in his hands to rinse her off, wrung out the sponge, and set it and the soap on the floor beside the tub.

Now he pressed tightly up to Adara's back, his rigid cock nestled in the small of her back. He wrung out her wet hair and pushed it to one side, kissing her at the juncture of her neck and shoulder, as his hands came around to squeeze her breasts and tweak her nipples. She gasped and a little shudder ran through her. His stiff member throbbed in response.

"Kneel so I can wash the backs of your legs," Stellan murmured in Adara's ear. With the water taking up a goodly percentage of their weight, they could kneel on the stone tub floor without pain. As Adara knelt before him, Stellan took up the sponge again. He ran it around her buttocks, and down the backs of her thighs beneath the water. Still sitting, he moved backward to scrub her feet, eliciting a squirm. She was just a little ticklish. Then he squeezed out the sponge again, and returned it to the floor beside the tub.

Stellan got up onto his own knees, and ran his hands between Adara's buttocks to her slippery sex. She gasped and moaned as he inserted two fingers and began moving them back and forth. They were trying to keep it down – it was bad enough the two old gray guys knew what they were doing in here, without them hearing every word as well. But Adara said softly and urgently, "Fuck me, Stellan! I want your cock inside me, now!"

She didn't have to ask twice. He guided the tip of his quivering member between her lips, and all the way home, with a low moan of his own. Oh, that felt so right! With all they'd been going through the past few... days, or whatever you could call them... Adara's body had been on his mind most of the time. What *was* it with her? He ached for her whenever they were apart, even if it was only by a few feet. And when they were together, he couldn't get enough!

He pounded into her, slower at first then faster and faster. Ungh, he wanted to cum. But the issue of doing so in the bathtub... He pulled out, slowly, and drew Adara around to face him. She crawled forward, wrapping her arms and legs around him, and slipping back down onto his throbbing member. They stayed that way in a tight embrace, kissing passionately, then she began to move up and down on him. The water made it nearly effortless.

She was close to coming herself when Stellan gripped her tightly and murmured into her ear, "I don't think we want to be bathing in cum." Mm, good point... Adara pulled off of him regretfully, and rose to her feet. Then she climbed out, dripping onto the carpet. This room had another of the brightly-colored, silken rugs that were in every other room of the apartment except the kitchen.

She gazed at Stellan hungrily, urging him to get out of the tub too. In moments he was standing before her, engulfing her in another deep embrace. Hmm, the carpet seemed soft enough, but... He plucked their towels off the hooks and laid them out atop the rug, then beckoned to Adara to lie down. She wrapped her legs around his hips as he entered her again, seizing her mouth in a deep kiss as his cock began moving in and out slowly and shallowly, then faster and

157

deeper until they exploded together at last in an awe-inspiring climax.

It was quite some time before the two humans emerged from the bathroom, clean and pink. They changed into some comfortable lounging clothes, and Stellan pooled the contents of the party's four packs to produce a meal of sorts. He discovered that a flat metal surface set into the stone counter in the kitchen would glow hot when you pressed the stud set into the wall, and was able to create a sort of stew from a mix of Siiri and kobold ingredients. In consideration of their companions' preference for bland foods, he left out the spices. But he was eagerly looking forward to some real human food in the near future.

The lights in the apartment brightened while they were eating, announcing that "day" had arrived in Zabran Lokaini. "As you above divide the time it takes from sun to sun into twenty-four hours," Ghryzindion explained, "so the Siiri still use the time-keeping devices they had when they were surface dwellers. They consider three to be a sacred number, and have decided that one-third of the time should be the time of darkness and sleep, with the other two-thirds devoted to work and leisure. Now that their labors are so few, I believe it is mostly the latter. If you are tired, you may wish to sleep now. After you have rested, we will have some hours in which to plot our strategy before lightfall comes again."

Adara and Stellan had laid out their cloaks atop the mattress in the bedroom, finding it a great deal more cushy and comfortable than the metal spring mattress they'd enjoyed in the former quarters of the Karindi queen. They were naked, she lying with her head on his shoulder and her left arm draped over his torso, gently playing her fingers through his mat of dark chest hair.

Adara was feeling much restored after the bath, the soul-stirring sex, and the meal. But now, as she thought about the last stage of their quest, her fears were beginning to stir. "Are you sorry you came with me?" she asked softly. "There certainly didn't turn out to be much plunder..." Stellan squeezed her and planted a kiss on her silken head, catching a whiff of the perfumed soap she'd used to wash her hair with.

"It's not all about plunder, Dari," he answered quietly.

She sought his eyes with her own, gazing into their black depths. "I'm worried about tomorrow," she admitted. "I'm protected from magic spells, and my irilium plate should protect me from the Belurii's weapons. But they're so well-armored themselves, it's going to be very hard to stop them. What happens if I kill their 'Leader' and then they go berserk? And if as Ghryzindion says the Mothers are linked to their tribespeople, won't the kobolds all go on the rampage against the Siiri once they learn the threat has been ended?"

Stellan kissed her on the lips this time, returning her gaze seriously. "Even after Chtorias is dead, the Mothers will still be under threat from the Belurii," he mused. "But they can call on their people for aid against the soldiers, and the soldiers' magical enhancements should be gone along with the sorcerer who created them – shouldn't they?"

"And Ghryzindion should be able to stop the Belurii, or at least some of them, with his spells," he went on. Adara kissed him back.

"You're right," she said. "I should just stop worrying and get some sleep." "Sleep?" Stellan responded, squeezing her tighter. "Who said I was going to let you go to sleep?"

Chapter 26

After catching close to eight hours of sleep, undisturbed by the still-somewhat-dim lights in the bedroom, Adara and Stellan made love again before rising. Who knew, it might be their last chance ever. She shoved the thought aside angrily. Try as she might to control her feelings, even with his reserve making it easier for her to hold back, the way she felt when she considered the possibility of Stellan dying told her it was no use – she'd lost her heart again.

But if he'd lost his heart to her, there was no sign of it. Not once had he said "I love you," not even in the heat of passion. It was clear he was "in lust" with Adara, but when that wore off would anything be left? Time would tell. She steeled herself for the likelihood that this lover, like the last one, would move on when their quest together was done.

They all breakfasted on more of the Siiri snack mix, Adara wishing for some hot tea to wash it down with. After eating they gathered in the living area, using their bedrolls for seats, to confer about their plans for lightfall. Ghryzindion took charge of the discussion.

"The Leader's Compound is the only area of Zabran Lokaini that has but one door connecting it with the rest of the city," he explained. "Before the rise of Chtorias, and his re-establishment of the ancient order of the Belurii who helped him achieve dominion here, the area was the largest of the city's many plazas. He had all of its connecting corridors walled off save one, protected by stout doors, and built a barracks, offices, and luxurious apartments within the circular space, accessed by a circular corridor with doors leading to the various areas on its inner wall."

"Do all the Belurii sleep there?" Adara asked, imagining that must get crowded.

"No, only the members of the Leader's Guard actually live there," the kobold shaman replied. "I visited the place on several occasions during my years as a trader before the coup. Recruits are trained there, and orders are sent out from there; but the majority of the Belurii, after their training is completed and they have been sworn into the order, will take up jobs as law enforcers – patrolling whatever area they are assigned to and living in quarters near to their patrol routes."

Adara heaved a sigh of relief. "So we're not going to run into the entire membership there," she said, and Ghryzindion nodded.

"Even among the Guard, most should be asleep when we arrive there. You must have realized, these people have had very little to fight for many centuries. The incursions of occasional parties of Karindi, seeking to free their fellow Kier Ludzi, have been very nearly their only excitement in ages."

"Are the Siiri a particularly law-abiding people?" Stellan asked out of curiosity. It was so hard to imagine those effete-looking, foppish elves forming a criminal underworld. Yet the number of Belurii patrols seemed to suggest that law enforcement was needed.

"Not nearly so much as are the Kier Ludzi," the old shaman replied. "Our biology knits us tightly together within our tribes, and we have no need of police. The Siiri will often seek personal advantage against their fellows, in contravention of the laws. But most of them are not guilty of anything worse than a little petty larceny."

And now we've brought murder to their door, Adara thought sadly. It particularly bothered her that she'd had to kill that kobold clerk – a man who'd clearly been terrified. The Belurii patrolmen had at least been armed and armored, and had a fighting chance.

"Will the rods we captured work on the Belurii?" Adara asked. The idea of just paralyzing their enemies and leaving them alive had a certain appeal.

"I am not certain," Ghryzindion admitted. "Likely they are a product of Chtorias' arts, and he may well have given their wielders an immunity to their effects. But certainly it's been demonstrated that my own spell of paralysis will work on them."

"Is that something you could teach me?" she asked. "I'm a quick learner." The old shaman snorted.

"I doubt the gods of the Kier Ludzi would grant you their powers, young hu-man. I studied for nearly a century to be able to cast the spell of paralysis, building up the strength of my conduit to the gods." Damn, Adara thought. Paralysis seemed to be a popular spell in many different magic systems – Sarand Bloodspire had used a similar spell on Ferdyn. Maybe, once they got through this, she should seek out someone to teach her some spellcraft.

Adara briefly considered lending the Darkshield to Ghryzindion. He was the only one among them with significant magical powers, the one most likely to succeed in their quest – provided he wasn't just knocked out of the fight with a spell. But she had worn the Darkshield almost all of her life, and while she felt she could probably trust the old kobold to return it, the reluctance to part with it was too strong. Might that be part of its magic? Perhaps it could only be given to a loved one, permanently.

They discussed strategies and contingencies for more hours, ate again, and then girded up to leave just a little before the anticipated lights-out. They wanted to meet as few people as possible on the trip between here and the Leader's Compound; but there was one they *hoped* to meet. And the chances of doing that after lightfall were small.

Even before they opened the door of the apartment, Adara quested out again to see what living things were stirring in their vicinity. There was no one in this corridor, but not far off she could detect a pattern of movement. Clusters of sentients were moving in groups, filing down corridors and going into dwellings. Most of the Siiri citizens would long since have been at home by this close to lightfall, but the kobold workers bunked in dormitories and would be on the job for most of the "day" before being allowed to return to their beds.

Adara found one of the colorful little lizards clinging to the wall of a nearby corridor and took in the scene. Yes, the people moving along this corridor were kobold workers. She briefly inhabited the minds of a succession of small creatures down the corridor in the direction the people were walking, and discovered a large underground chamber. It looked nothing like the quarters of the Karindas tribe, but neither was it as ornately decorated as most of the areas of Zabran Lokaini she'd seen so far.

The room was lined with stone beds covered with thin pallets, and at the far end of it a food preparation area was in operation. The workers were lining up to receive their evening rations, eating together at long metal tables. Definitely, this was one of the residence areas for the kobold slaves. She saw no Siiri overseers or Belurii among them. Apparently the threat of death to the tribes' pomatkas was enough to keep the captives in line, at least most of the time. "I found a dormitory," Adara reported. "It's off a long corridor crossing the one outside the door here, away in that direction." She gestured, and Ghryzindion nodded.

"We will head in that direction now," he said. "But stay alert for patrols." Stellan relocked the apartment door behind them, and they set off in the direction Adara had indicated. Once again she had the difficult task of moving on her feet with her mind in two places at once; but she felt hugely refreshed by their hours of rest and recreation.

As they reached the crossing corridor, they hung back within the deserted one while Adara scanned it in the direction opposite the one that led to the dormitory. All of the traffic along here seemed to be flowing toward the dormitory, but the crowds of a few minutes ago had diminished to a trickle. Lightfall would come soon.

Occupying the mind of a lizard, Adara peered at the figure that was approaching. The little scaly creature was somewhat nearsighted, needing mostly to see and identify insects that were within the range of his tongue. But she could make out that the approaching person was definitely alone, and definitely not Siiri. She nodded to Ghryzindion, and he stepped out into the corridor to block the coming kobold's path.

They'd gone around and around on this issue, after the fiasco with the clerk. Adara supplied her opinion that the clerk had probably been born here and never known any other way of life, which had led to him siding with his masters; and the old shaman had had to agree. The plan now was to approach a worker. If he reacted in terror, he would be paralyzed and they would simply relieve him of his clothes and leave him locked in one of the storerooms along this quiet corridor. They could let him out again before he starved, provided they were successful in their quest.

It turned out not to be an issue. When the old kobold shaman stepped out into the still brightly-lit corridor to confront the approaching worker, he stared in astonishment. "Clazhindon! Is it you?" he gasped. The other was struck speechless for a moment, taking in this apparition from the past. Finally, he murmured

"Ghryzindion. It cannot be!" They were speaking in kobold, but Adara and Stellan could tell that the four of them had just been handed an unbelievable stroke of luck.

"Quickly, into this corridor before anyone else comes!" the shaman commanded, and his old acquaintance obeyed. He could not imagine how it should be that his fellow trader, a Karindi he had thought long dead, should be standing here in the depths of Zabran Lokaini dressed as an old-fashioned shaman.

Clazhindon's huge, pale blue eyes widened still more when he saw the party waiting a few feet down the corridor. He thought he recognized Brzhandin, but were those two tall warriors hu-mans? He had not met any in seven hundred years, more than half his life ago; but he could not imagine what else they would be. Their eyes were not those of the udur.

Adara found them another empty apartment, this one considerably less well-appointed than the one in which they'd slept; and soon Stellan had let them into it where they could confer without fear of discovery. The lights dimmed to a faint glow soon after they came inside.

In Franca, Ghryzindion told his human companions, "This is my old colleague Clazhindon, of the Inziras tribe. He was just a youngster, no more than four or five hundred years old, when Chtorias staged his coup and the profession of trader went extinct." To the younger kobold he added, "You still remember your Franca, I hope."

Clazhindon nodded, figuring things out. In the same language he replied "I have forgotten nothing, though it has been a long time. I still miss bacon!" The old shaman snorted in laughter. "Me too. What have they got you doing, these days?" The former trader shrugged. "Working in food production, below. At least I always get enough to eat. But tell me, Ghryzindion, how is it you are here? And a shaman? We all thought the Karindi were destroyed, killed off by the Belurii centuries ago."

They were seated on a stone bench that seemed to be the apartment's only furnishing, while Adara and Stellan had sat down cross-legged atop their cloaks on the floor and Brzhandin remained standing. The old one shook his head sadly. "That is very nearly the case," he admitted. "Only eighteen of the Karindi yet live, back within our tribal home. Our shaman's apprentice was one killed during the fight after they slew our pomatka, and as I no longer had an occupation I was chosen to take his place. Alas, I did not receive my full training before my mistress died. But I get by. Am I right in thinking that there are no more shamans among the Kier Ludzi?"

His friend nodded. "The Belurii killed most, and the staffs were destroyed," he said. "A few remain who have learned the teachings, but without the staff they can cast no spells. Chtorias is not happy with competition even from among his own people. He provided the Belurii patrols with those paralysis rods, which he enchanted himself. But the study and practice of the magical arts is not allowed within Zabran Lokaini at all. It is rumored there are at least a few magi or other sorcerers among the Siiri, but if so they are keeping out of sight."

Hmm, Adara thought. Another megalomaniacal magic user, setting himself up as a ruler and trampling over people's lives. She hoped the lack of magical assistance was going to bite Chtorias on the ass. "No doubt you're wondering why we are here, Clazhindon?" Ghryzindion asked. His friend gave a wry smile, an unlikely expression on those blunt gray features.

"I think I can guess," he said casually.

Chapter 27

Belurii headquarters was in turmoil, and though lightfall had been more than two hours ago patrols were still going out into the city in four times their usual numbers, milling about in the circular corridor surrounding the Leader's Compound as they were issued their assignments and then hustling out again.

The Leader's Guard, whose responsibility it was to guard the entrance to the compound, had doubled that force for the night shift. There wasn't room for everyone to stand on station, and some of the extras just positioned themselves a few feet along the corridor on either side of the doors, in a state of high alert.

Two of their own had been slain! Brutally slaughtered, along with a hapless kobold clerk from a food distribution center miles from here. The bodies had been discovered just before lightfall, though a search had been on for the missing men for more than a full day. Who or what could have done such a thing? With their paralysis rods, their beautiful and effective irilium armor, and the finest blades known to the udur – and therefore, obviously, the finest blades in the world – it seemed impossible that a team of Belurii should have been defeated.

Commander Debindias postulated that it must have been a large invading force that had somehow managed to avoid being seen, and insisted that patrols would now consist of eight, not two, Belurii. Many from among the Leader's Guard had been conscripted to fill out these enlarged patrols, leaving the barracks almost empty.

Lieutenant Commander Marisias was in charge of the doubled guard on the gates, and the anxiety and confusion were beginning to wear him down. He was supposed to be asleep in his comfortable bed at this hour, not riding herd on a mismatched guard squad who had never worked together before. Half of them had never even stood night duty on the gates until now.

Things had been exciting back in the days when the Leader was seizing power, and again when the influx of kobolds had arrived; but he'd been a lowly recruit back then, still in training, and had not had any responsibilities beyond obeying the orders of his superiors. Now, he worried: what if this "large invading force" of unknown composition somehow slipped past the patrols and attacked the gate? Would his men hold?

An hour later things had settled down considerably. The last of the augmented patrols had been sent out, each assigned to an area of the city, and the dozen guarding the gates were feeling let down. Few things were more deflating than to be whipped into a state of high excitement – only to then have to stand motionless for an hour or more, with nothing to do but stare in the direction from which danger might come.

The corridor ahead of them was dim and deserted, and they were beginning to relax – pacing around, drinking from canteens, conversing with their teammates. Then suddenly they all went on the alert again as pounding feet could be heard coming down the corridor. But it was only one set of feet – surely nothing to fear?

The figure appeared, gasping for breath – one of the kobold workers, all of whom (save the small force of night shift workers in the food production facilities below) should have long since been in their beds. The kobolds all looked pretty much alike to the Siiri – rough-hewn, brutish figures with no grace or sophistication. But Marisias could tell this was one of the old guard, someone who'd been an adult when he came here, by the way he butchered the graceful, lilting Siiri tongue with his barbarous accent.

"Intruders!" he gasped, after bowing formally to the Belurii officer. An electric thrill shot through Marisias. Those they sought had been found!

"Where, and how many? How are they armed?" he demanded, though he doubted this gray lout would know one weapon from another. The fact that his people had often traded for weapons made by the kobolds was something he preferred to forget.

"In Food Sector Green," the kobold got out, though he was still evidently in a panic and panting for breath.

"You're one of the night workers there?" Marisias demanded, and the kobold nodded.

"I was in the processing facility when they came in, probably from the stairs over in the Tourmaline District," he explained. Rather than numbers, the Siiri preferred to assign visual names to the areas of their city. The living levels all had districts named after gems, and the food production areas below after colors.

"I asked you how many!" the officer thundered, and though he could have picked the fop up and thrown him twenty feet without any strain, Clazhindon cringed.

"Sorry, sir! There were six of them, all tall and thin and dressed like Belurii. The light was dim, but I think they might have been pinudur!"

Marisias' golden complexion paled to a sickly yellow. Pinudur! It was the men settling in this part of Eorla who had driven the Siiri to abandon the sun above for safety below, not their fellow elves. But where mankind had long since forgotten that the aurudur existed, it was likely the pinudur still remembered. Might this be a raid, seeking plunder? These corridors had not seen any pinudur in more than a thousand years, but the memories of the udur were long.

Putting a name and face to the mysterious intruders had relieved a lot of Marisias' anxiety, despite learning that they were well-armored. A mere six pinudur could surely not stand against a larger force of Belurii! "What were their weapons?" he demanded.

The cowering kobold replied, "They had gleaming longswords and daggers, sir. But they also had some of those rods the patrolmen carry. They paralyzed me and I was unable to move for several minutes. Then I ran here as soon as I could!"

Yes, the two dead patrolmen's paralysis rods had been taken. Now, more than ever, Marisias was sure that this gray worm was telling the truth. Hastily, he called the five extra members of the gate guard to him. "You five, come with me! This worker is going to lead us to where the intruders were seen, and we'll pick up one of the eight-man patrols on the way. Jenas, you've got command of the gate guard until I return! We'll bring back the bodies of this pinudur raiding party with us, for the Leader to see!"

Clazhindon smiled grimly to himself as he took the lead, the six heavily-armed Belurii following him like would-be consorts in pursuit of a pomatka. It was a little over a mile to the stairs leading down to Food Sector Green, and once they were there these Leader's Guard members would find themselves in completely unfamiliar territory. The imaginary party of pinudur could have gone almost

168

anywhere in the labyrinthine lower level by then, and he would lead his escort a merry chase for as long as it took. He surely hoped, though, that it would not be long.

Chapter 28

Adara had been tracking the activity near the gates to the Leader's Compound remotely, following the spark that was Clazhindon as he rushed down the corridor, conferred with a spark she assumed was the guard commander, and then joined with five more sparks to rush away from the gates and down a side corridor – moving in a hurry. Six more sparks remained by the gates, and there were many more sentients within the living areas of the Compound itself; but it appeared they now had a more manageable number of guards to deal with.

The four conferred hurriedly in whispers, then came out of a side corridor and began creeping in the dim light down toward the gates. Stellan held one of the paralysis rods, Brzhandin the other; but it was Ghryzindion in the lead. One of the more alert guards spotted movement in the corridor ahead, and called out to them, "Halt! Who goes there?" The old shaman sent his spell of paralysis at the speaker, even as the other men activated their rods.

The rods did nothing. The targeted guards didn't drop, but came rushing down the corridor as soon as the one who'd called out had fallen to the kobold shaman's spell. They had their swords out. Evidently the Leader's Guard were not issued paralysis rods as part of their normal equipment. Those did seem more like a policing tool than a warrior's weapon.

Stellan tucked the useless rod into his belt and drew his sword, just as the foremost of the approaching guards suddenly collapsed – a second victim of the old shaman's spell. He knew full well what it felt like to be the subject of that spell, the utter frustration of remaining awake while being unable to move a single muscle. Only heartbeat, respiration, and the involuntary blinking of eyes would be possible until the spell wore off.

Brzhandin, too, tucked his rod away and drew a weapon – one they hadn't seen him wield before. He had carried many things in that heavy pack of his. This was a hardened steel warhammer – not a pretty weapon, but a massively heavy one with a handle some three feet in length. It appeared to have been forged, head and shaft, from a single bar of metal.

All six of the remaining gate guards had left their post to rush the intruders, and four of them were still on their feet. Using both hands and all that massive kobold strength, Brzhandin stepped forward and swung the hammer as hard as he could. It took the nearest Belurii guard, who was approximately the same height as his opponent, in the side of the neck where the relatively delicate bevor came up beneath the overhang of the helmet. It crashed right through the armor, and the attacker fell with a broken neck.

Meanwhile Adara and Stellan had rushed around the three remaining guards to come at them from the rear – trapping them between two forces of enemies and distracting their attention from the relatively unarmed Ghryzindion. One of them whirled as Stellan's sword found a weak point in his armor, stabbing him in the back of the knee. It was certainly not a fatal blow, but it hurt like hell. As he looked up, wondering how even a kobold could have mistaken this tall, thin human for a pinudur, he suddenly found himself lying on the floor as the paralysis spell took hold.

Now there were only two. Before Ghryzindion could paralyze any more of them, Brzhandin took out a second one with his warhammer. If you had the muscle to wield it, it was clearly an ideal weapon against these warriors in their irilium plate. The last one, distracted when his companion fell howling in pain with a broken shoulder, let Adara slip past his guard and plunge Voleur's point into his throat just above the bevor. He collapsed to the floor, choking on his own blood.

Breathing hard, Adara gazed in consternation at the bodies sprawled in the corridor. The good news was that none of her own party were hurt, and the gates to the Leader's Compound now stood unguarded. The bad news was that these men, even the ones who were as yet alive and uninjured, were going to have to die.

She turned away, head down, as Ghryzindion and Brzhandin set about breaking the necks of the guards who weren't already dead. Stellan came up beside her and put an arm across her armored back. "It's war, Dari," he said softly. "I'm sorry, but that's how it has to be." She nodded sadly. When and why, she wondered, had he picked up this pet name he'd suddenly started using? Might his feelings for her be deeper than he'd shown?

"That was some amazing sword work, by the way," he added a little more cheerfully. "Remind me not to piss you off." She gave him a wry grin, and set about helping the kobolds to pick up the bodies and carry them off. There was something like a broom closet off the corridor they'd been hiding in, half-full of implements for cleaning; and they packed the slender Siiri corpses in like cordwood. The door had no lock, but they could hope that with all the excitement in Zabran Lokaini tonight nobody would be going in there after brooms and mops.

The gates leading to the circular corridor surrounding the Leader's Compound did have locks, though – and a sturdy bar as well. They'd found a set of keys on one of the guards' bodies, and after going inside the compound they were able to lock the gates tight behind them. "Ghryzindion, do you have a locking spell that would work to prevent these gates from being opened by someone with lockpicks or a key?" Adara asked. She'd seen him use something like that on doors a couple of times since they'd met.

"Good idea, Adara," the old shaman said, and applied his staff to the locking mechanisms. "Until I remove the spell, these locks will not open again," he assured them. "However if someone uses axes on the doors, the spell will do nothing to prevent them from being splintered. I suggest we move swiftly, before any of those patrols come back."

After affixing the bar the party stood in the corridor, peering down the long curve of it in either direction. Lights were dim here as well, and there was no one in sight. Adara guessed that everyone who lived here must now be sleeping. "The Belurii headquarters are down around that side," Ghryzindion told them as he gestured to their left. "I visited here a few times, around eight to nine hundred years ago. I have no idea where they are keeping the Mothers, but I feel sure that we will find Chtorias' private apartment down in this other direction." He led them off to the right, all of them moving as silently as possible on the polished stone floor.

As they walked widdershins around the circle the wall to their right appeared to be a continuous circle, with a beautiful abstract mural covering its surface. The ceiling was higher than in most normal corridors, and Adara recalled that his area had once been a plaza. On their left, they occasionally came on closed doors. The doors, and the wall they were set into, were covered in more of the traditional Siiri ornamentation – beautiful, but devoid of any emotional content beyond a generalized sense of peace and warmth.

Suddenly they came upon a pair of double doors, the first such they'd seen opening off this corridor. Adara stared in fascination. In all their time spent in Zabran Lokaini, there had been no sign of representational art. "I think we've found the Leader's quarters," she said softly. "And I think I know what he looks like." Blazoned across the left-hand door, rendered in the glowing mineral pigments favored by the Siiri, was the face of an astonishingly beautiful golden-skinned man with hair like a silken rainbow and eyes like the pits of Hell.

Chapter 29

Adara cast out her awareness, then reported in a whisper "No one is moving around the circle. And in a room behind these doors and off to the right there are two sentients. Ah, and there is a small creature, maybe a pet?"

"The Siiri brought little furred creatures with them when they came underground," Ghryzindion confirmed. "Can you use it to see?"

The creature had been sleeping, curled up in a ball atop a cushion in a corner of the presumed bedchamber. Adara gently nudged it awake while preventing it from making a sound, and peered around. The illumination inside the sleeping chamber was even dimmer than that in the corridor, but the creature (something like a weasel, she thought, from what she could see of its body) seemed to have eyes well adapted for seeing in low light.

At her commanding suggestion the creature arose silently from its bed and moved around the apartment. There was a room immediately behind the double doors, which appeared to be a sitting room. Out a door beyond it was an opulent bathroom, putting the facilities they'd enjoyed recently to shame. And the room the little animal had been sleeping in appeared to be the Leader's bedchamber. Two figures slumbered in an enormous bed. One was likely Chtorias, the other smaller – his mistress?

Adara sent her furry little spy back to sleep on its pillow, then reported her findings to her companions. They exchanged glances, then nodded in silent agreement and approached the doors. Unsurprisingly, they were locked. Stellan bent to the lock with his picks in hand, as Adara wondered: would the sorcerer be paranoid enough to use magic to secure the door to his quarters, even though he has a huge cadre of deadly, loyal warriors guarding him?

He would not. And while the Siiri seemed to be miles ahead of the humans above in some areas of household technology, they didn't seem to have made any improvements to their locks in millennia. With a grin, Stellan felt the third and last tumbler click over and lightly lifted the latch. The door swung silently open.

The carpets were thick, the most luxuriant they'd yet encountered. But no matter how quietly the four entered the apartment, the little creature Adara had ridden a few minutes before came alert. Before it could raise an alarm, she sent it back into a deep sleep with a firm, irresistible command.

"Better lock the door again," she breathed to Stellan, and he nodded. In another couple of minutes the door was once again locked, and at a nod from Adara the old shaman applied his spell of reinforcement. Now, weapons at the ready, the party made their way toward the bedroom. Ghryzindion was in the lead, ready to drop their quarry with his paralysis spell. Once he was helpless, they could dispose of him at their leisure.

As he stepped through the doorway, the room was suddenly a blaze of light. The old kobold shaman barely had time to see, pupils contracted to pinpoints and his vision almost blown out by the unaccustomed glare, that only a small Siiri woman lay in the bed. Behind him, his three companions only knew that they had just stepped into trouble.

The Siiri sorcerer Chtorias, hiding in the corner beside the door, cast a spell of obedience on the kobold intruder before stepping out into the room to get a look at the party who had broken into his quarters. He had immediately recognized Ghryzindion as an old-time kobold shaman, a breed he thought he had eradicated centuries before. No Belurii had returned from the home of the Karindi to tell the tale of what had happened there.

What a bizarre party! The old shaman, clearly well past his fifteenth century; a kobold warrior little younger; and two tall, slender, armored figures he took to be pinudur or perhaps humans. Why in all the hells were they here? "Paralyze your companions," Chtorias instructed, and Ghryzindion obediently raised his staff. He first hit Brzhandin, in the act of raising his warhammer. Then he felled Stellan, and by now there was a loud pounding at the door and voices on the other side of it shouting in the burbling Siiri tongue.

Adara scrambled to evade the kobold shaman's aim. The spell, it appeared, was cast through the staff – and the staff must be pointing at its intended target. That seemed an inefficient technique. Should not the spell be aimed by the mind of its caster? But she knew nothing of how kobold magic worked, only that she needed to get into the next room. How had Chtorias managed to be lying in wait for them, when he had been asleep only moments before they came in? And how had he summoned whatever guards still remained within the compound?

Dodging left and right while rushing toward the doorway, Adara got inside Ghryzindion's guard and struck him a glancing blow on the forehead with the hilt of Voleur before knocking him to the ground. Then she confronted the Siiri sorcerer. For half a second, she wasn't sure whether she wanted to cleave him with her sword – or have him do the same for her.

He stood naked, and though he must be well over a millennium old he looked as though he might be in his early twenties. That devastatingly beautiful face with its glowing, deep orange eyes was accompanied by a body so perfect it took her breath away. His skin was the same slightly-glowing golden color all over, utterly smooth and hairless except for the fine rainbow-colored silken strands on his head. His dangling member, unaccompanied by pubic hair, was considerably larger than one might expect for a man who stood three inches shorter than she did. From his broad, muscular shoulders to his narrow hips, Chtorias was the embodiment of a somewhat-undersized god.

The sorcerer and the Darkshield bearer confronted one another from a distance of three feet across the now brightly-lit room, mouths open in surprise. It was a woman! Chtorias realized, and hurled his own spell of paralysis – since apparently she'd managed to knock out his recently-acquired thrall. Adara felt the Darkshield tingle, in a way that was familiar from the time a few days ago in the ancient kobold king's tomb. With a pang of regret, she swung Voleur straight and true – severing the Siiri sorcerer's head from his shoulders.

Chapter 30

There was an appalling amount of blood, and a hysterical Siiri woman who had abruptly woken up at the moment that Chtorias' head had fallen to the room's luxuriant carpet. And Adara did not have a single word in common with her. She hastily pulled out a spare shirt from her pack and wiped off Voleur's blade, then sheathed it.

Behind her, Stellan and Brzhandin were out for the count – unless maybe Ghryzindion could reverse his spell. He was beginning to moan and stir on the carpet in the doorway, coming around after the blow to the head and (she had to assume, and pray) no longer under any compulsion. When the sorcerer had appeared and the kobold shaman had done his bidding, Adara had known in an instant what had happened. She'd witnessed sorcerous compulsion before.

Adara tore off her helmet and flung it to the side, so that the woman could see she was also a woman, and that she was not threatening. "There, there," she said soothingly. "It's all right, I'm not going to hurt you. Sorry about your boyfriend there, but… you know, you reap what you sow."

Her words had no effect on the woman, who was a still-smaller and even more lovely version of the basic Siiri model. She had small round breasts, a somewhat pointed chin that emphasized her elfin features, and eyes that shown like pools of iridescence – first one color, then another. She soon had the blanket pulled up to her shoulders, and a wordless keening was issuing from her lips as tears fell from her limpid eyes and made Adara feel like a first-class shit.

Going nowhere on that front, Adara turned to Ghryzindion and helped him up onto his feet. "Sorry I had to hit you," she said, and he shook his head. He picked his staff up off the floor and waved it a bit, and suddenly the bloody abrasion Voleur's hilt had left on his bald pate closed up and faded into invisibility. A look of sharp awareness came into his pale blue eyes.

"What happened?" the old shaman grated, looking first at the bloody headless corpse on the carpet near the foot of the bed and then at the cowering woman. The pet, which resembled an oversized version of an ermine, had left its pillow and was now hiding inside the room's closet.

"I think Chtorias cast some kind of compulsion on you," Adara told him. Apparently, this version of the spell didn't leave the target with memories of what had occurred while they were under its influence. "You zapped Brzhandin and Stellan, but I ducked out of the way. I didn't want the sorcerer to realize I was immune to magic until I could get closer to him."

Both of them became aware of a pounding on the doors to the apartment, and more shouts in the Siiri tongue. "He must have had a telepathic link to the guards, perhaps through an enchanted amulet," Ghryzindion said. Oh, that would explain it.

"Likely it won't be long before they bring axes," Adara remarked. "Can you un-paralyze Stellan and Brzhandin, and maybe try to get Miss Whatsername over there calmed down? Her screaming is starting to get on my nerves."

The old shaman's face took on a grim smile. He gestured with his staff, and their two companions began stirring. Then he turned to the exquisitely lovely and extremely hysterical woman in the bed, speaking to her in the Siiri tongue. She seemed to calm almost immediately, and spoke with him for another minute or so.

"Wow, what did you say to her?" Adara asked.

"I told her that we intended her no harm, and that we were only here to free the Kier Ludzi from bondage," he explained. "I also hit her with a spell of my own. It's not exactly compulsion, but it has a way of making its object… more amenable to reason, you might say. I invoked her sympathy for her fellow women, and asked her for the location of the part of the Compound where the Mothers are kept. They are to be found behind another set of double doors, not that far along the corridor in the direction we were going earlier."

That was great. Now they just needed to get past an unknown number of guards in the corridor outside, and the Kier Ludzi were home free. Well, free at least. Home was going to take some doing. Then another thought occurred to Adara. The Mothers!
"Ghryzindion, since I killed Chtorias the Mothers have been freed from his compulsion, right?" she asked. The old kobold nodded.
"They're communicating with their tribes telepathically then?" He

nodded again, his face showing that he was following her line of thought.

"They are still locked up. Won't they be telling their people to arise, to take up arms and strike down their Siiri oppressors?" Adara asked. Ghryzindion nodded.

"That is likely," he said.

"But most of the Siiri people were as much in thrall to Chtorias as they were!" she protested. "It would be a senseless slaughter! We need to get out there and tell them to stop the violence, to let their people's transition to freedom be a peaceful one."

The old shaman considered her words, then nodded. "You are right," he said. "It is not the Siiri people who conspired to place my people in bondage, but that pile of refuse that now lies in two pieces on the carpet. And thank you for that, by the way. But how are we to reach the Mothers with this request when a horde of guards is outside the door?"

Stellan and Brzhandin were now fully recovered from the paralysis spell, and came through into the room to see the corpse of Chtorias draining the last of its blood onto the once-lovely carpet. "How many of them are out there, Adara?" Stellan asked, and she quickly checked.

"There's not that many of them" Adara reported after a brief scan. "I think that the majority of the Leader's Guard must have been drafted for those extra-large patrols. I count six, no – seven, sentients in the hallway outside the doors." And from the sound of it, they were bringing axes.

"Grandfather, can you cast your spell of 'amenability' through the doors?" Adara asked. She had truly come to think of the old kobold shaman as a respected elder, somebody whose judgment she trusted. Ghryzindion gave her a full-on grin, and gestured with his staff toward the doorway. Though the magic of the kobolds appeared to require aiming with the staff, his mystic senses were seemingly able to pinpoint the targets without seeing them. Go kobold gods!

In moments the pounding had ceased, and Ghryzindion raised his voice in the Siiri tongue that sounded to Adara's ears like the burbling of water in a small brook. His command of that language was apparently as superb as his command of Franca – clearly he was a man in a thousand among his kind. And the guards on the other side of those doors drank up what he had to say, with little in the way of argument.

Chapter 31

The key turned in the lock, and the right-hand door to the quarters of the kobold Mothers opened. The fact that all of them had been sleeping when they were suddenly released from Chtorias' centuries-old spell of command (delivered originally via the jeweled spheres, but still linked to the living sorcerer) meant that most of them had not awakened but had merely transitioned into strange dreams. Three of the twenty-nine had gotten up from their beds and were sitting in the communal dining room where they took their meals, discussing the strange feeling that had come over them, when the doors were opened to admit Ghryzindion – accompanied by his teammates and the remaining complement of Leader's Guard Belurii.

It was the very threat of mass slaughter, initiated by the freed kobold Mothers and carried out by their tribespeople, that had decided the issue for Commander Debindias. The kobold slaves, including many whose daily work involved picks, shovels, and other potential weapons, outnumbered the Belurii by at least four to one. And while they might not be armored, each of them possessed far more strength than even the doughtiest Siiri warrior could muster.

Their Leader was dead. And with him had died all of his spells. The paralysis rods still functioned, it seemed – but many of the Belurii's sorcerous enhancements had failed. The kobold shaman's proposal, that the Belurii should allow the captive kobolds and their pomatkas to leave peaceably, had seemed like the best possible outcome to this disaster. And Debindias had not needed Ghryzindion's spell to reach that conclusion.

The old shaman addressed them in the tongue of the Kier Ludzi, dazzled at the effect their mere presence had on them. The freemartins of his people were technically female, but they were colleagues and equals. These pomatkas were objects of desire – a desire that affected any healthy adult male of his race. He had never had the opportunity to become a consort, and like the majority of his fellows he probably never would. But what need had an individual to breed, when he was surrounded by his brothers and sisters, nieces and nephews?

Yet the instinctive urge to do so was there, and none of the women in this sprawling apartment were related to him. He stifled the distracting feelings, and after making sure that all were now awake, addressed them. "I am Ghryzindion, once a trader and now shaman of what remains of the Karindi," he said. "With the help of my brother Brzhandin, and the two valiant humans Adara Willoughby and Stellan Archer, we have come to free the Kier Ludzi. Chtorias is dead, and you are now free of his compulsion. But we beg you, reach out to your people and command them to remain calm. Do not strike out at the Siiri, as they are a people of worth – and most of them did not take part in enslaving us."

The Mothers of the Kier Ludzi were awakening from a seven-hundred-year daze. As had been the case with the brief spell of compulsion Chtorias had cast on Ghryzindion, they had no clear memories of what had transpired during the time they had been enthralled. During all those centuries they had lived mostly content – coupling with their consorts, birthing children, always convinced that their lives here, confined in this small compound, were as they should be.

Being born a pomatka was no sure guarantee of possessing the other qualities needed in a ruling queen, and this was a flaw in the kobolds' way of doing things. Some were unable to deal with the realization that everything they'd believed for the past several centuries was the product of an evil magic spell. Others, more intelligent, were furious.

"All of the Siiri people conspired with the sorcerer to enslave us!" one insisted. Ghryzindion struggled with the desire to enfold her in his arms, so beautiful did she seem in her righteous anger.

"They were as much in thrall to Chtorias as you were," he insisted. This was not truly the case. The free labor provided by the captive kobolds had been a perk provided by the sorcerer to make his rule over his people more palatable, and they had accepted it. But he agreed with Adara that most of the Siiri, at least, had not truly held any malice. And *had* any thought that the enslavement of his people was wrong, there had been nothing any of them could do about it.

Adara, Stellan, and the small party of Leader's Guards stood aside, watching in fascination and incomprehension as the old kobold debated with the women who were the lifespring of his race in a language none of them knew. Adara at least could see the effect they were having on him, though it astounded her. There must be some pheromone given off by the pomatkas, to cause someone as old and wise as Ghryzindion to be brought nearly to his knees, hot with desire, merely by being in their presence. His mind might be old and wise, but he was fighting against bodily instincts any fifteen-year-old human boy would have understood.

Yet he persevered, and eventually he triumphed. During their long captivity, living in conditions so utterly different from the traditional ways of the Kier Ludzi, the Mothers had developed a hierarchy of their own – a pecking order based on the attributes of the individual pomatkas. It was the pomatka of the Gerandi, older than many and wiser than all the rest, who finally spoke for all of them.

"Very well, Ghryzindion," she said in a voice freighted with command. "You have convinced us. We will gather our tribes, and we will return with them to our homes – assuming those homes still exist. There will be no slaughter of the Siiri. But reparations will be required from them for the harm we have endured. And the Belurii must put down their arms."

Meanwhile outside the barred and magically locked gates of the compound, more axes had been found. When the negotiations were concluded, the remaining Leader's Guards hurriedly accompanied Ghryzindion to the entry gates. Those gates were sturdy, though, and not much progress had been made toward destroying them before the Belurii's supreme commander called out "Stop! This is Commander Debindias! We are opening the gates!" The pounding stopped, and the kobold shaman released his spell of binding. Then Debindias used his set of keys, and the gates swung open.

The corridor beyond was filled with Belurii, a mix of Leader's Guards and regular patrolmen. The cadre that had followed Clazhindon, and the eight-man patrol they'd picked up in their rush toward Food Sector Green, were still wandering lost in the corridors on the level below. Their kobold guide had long since slipped away from them.

183

Every kobold within Zabran Lokaini was now awake, and had picked up any tool that might be used as a weapon. They were even now making their ways through the miles of corridors toward the Leader's Compound, adjured by their queens not to attack any Siiri unless they themselves were attacked. As most of the non-military population of the city was asleep at this hour, there were few confrontations. By the time the lights went up again, the city was in kobold hands.

Chapter 32

They rounded one last bend in the mountain trail, and beheld the roofs of Feingeld beneath them. Ghryzindion's face fell as he caught sight of the town he had not visited in more than seven hundred years. He was wearing cunningly-fashioned metal goggles, antiques left over from the days when the kobolds traded above ground every year, to reduce the glare of daylight to a manageable level for his sensitive eyes. The other three kobolds in their party were similarly outfitted.

"What happened here?" he asked Adara. "Was there an avalanche?" She shook her head.

"Sorry, I'm afraid it was the disappearance of the kobold trade that caused Feingeld to die," she said. "It's so far up in the mountains, there was no real reason for people to live here once the gold mine was exhausted and your people no longer came."

The old kobold shaman, once a trader and planning to become one again, shook his head sadly. "I think we will give them until next year to resume trading, then," he said. He and his cohorts, as well as the three humans, were heavily laden with armor, weapons, and jewelry – but they had not brought it to trade. The items were gifts, their thanks to Adara and Stellan for their part in restoring the Kier Ludzi to freedom.

Miles behind and below them, the heart-place of the Karindi had become the new home of the Szendari. This tribe, one of the smaller ones, had also been the one whose heart-place was closest to Zabran Lokaini. The annexation and remodeling of the Szendaras tribe's home had been the first project the Siiri had put their captive workers to, and there was no trace remaining of their place as it once had been.

Ghryzindion, with the approval of the other nineteen members of the Karindi, had made the offer and it had been accepted: the pomatka of the Szendari would take one of the Karindi males as her consort, and any of the other Karindi who wished to would be adopted into the Szendaras tribe. They lacked the telepathic bond with her that the true-born Szendari had; but in time the children of the Szendari would be their blood relations.

She had chosen Brzhandin, and the deal was sealed. By the time she was ready to mate again, in another year, the move should have been completed. All of the Karindi freemartins and several of the Karindi males had agreed to join the new tribe. But other Karindi males besides Brzhandin had been offered the chance to become consorts. The Kier Ludzi Mothers were immensely grateful to the Karindi, last keepers of the flame, for all they had done to restore their race to its traditional way of life.

Adara heard a "Mraugh," and looked up to see wings silhouetted against the blue mountain sky. Malika fluttered down with a cony in her jaws, landing on all fours and folding her wings as she set about devouring her fat furry treat. During her time in the deep home of the kobolds Jaime had worked with her daily in the areas with higher ceilings, and she was now fully fledged. She seemed to have grown appreciably during the short time since she'd been rescued from certain death. But though she was now free to fly away and take up the life of a wild semigryph, she apparently didn't want to do so. She and Adara had bonded, and she regarded the woman as her "property."

Jaime and Arzhindin were walking together, conversing in a mix of kobold and Franca. The boy had become the Karindi's unofficial mascot during the time he'd spent with them. There had been no children in their tribe for hundreds of years, and the young human's perspective on the world had been refreshing. Each of them had been eager for a chance to converse with him, and to teach him what they knew. He'd now decided that while he might one day run Underhill Farm, he intended to become a trader and liaison with the Kier Ludzi. What other human, present company excepted, knew a tenth as much about them as he did?

They arrived in the town in mid-morning, and made their way to the Dragon's Head. The innkeeper peered at them in astonishment, though in the dimly-lit room he had not yet realized just how strange the party truly was. "You again!" he said. "I'd thought you lost in the mountains. I'm pretty sure it was your horses that Jurgen the goatherd brought in a couple of weeks ago."

"He did?" Adara's eyes lit. "Are they still here?" The innkeeper nodded.

"I've got them in the stables out back. I was going to try to sell them to my next hunting party if you didn't return soon. They're eating me out of fodder I'd expected to last for weeks. Jurgen said your party passed him on the high pasture, and then a few days later the horses showed up – no saddles or bridles, nothing but halters on them. They were happy to see him, and he had no trouble getting them to follow him back to town."

Without saddles or bridles, getting the horses and all their new baggage back to Willoughby was going to be a challenge. But Adara was very glad to know that Zarhya and Sadiq had not been eaten by snow lions. She happily paid over all the coin the innkeeper asked, and was delighted to learn he had some spare tack she could buy as well. It wasn't until all of this had been transacted that his gaze fell on the shorter, wider, grayer members of their party.

The innkeeper's face turned as pale as Ghryzindion's, as the old kobold stepped up to the bar and held out a hand. "Good day to you, sir," he said in nearly flawless Franca. "I am Ghryzindion, chief trader of the Szendaras tribe of the kobolds. This is a fine establishment you have here. Have you considered taking on a partner?"

The End
(for now…)